THEY WERE EXCELLENT TARGETS

Bonner opencd up, the big .50-caliber telegraphing its message—death—the weighty bullcts slamming into the Lightning squadsmen with fearful accuracy. The long white riding coats turned red.

A bike skidded across the road. An arrow exploded in the midst of a mass of men and machines. The first few bikes were doomed, and Bonner and Starling dispatched them quickly. But the snowmen were a disciplined group. The riders behind the leaders had slowed down and formcd up behind their fallen brethren. They had no clear idea of where Starling and Bonner stood, but they fired back round after round into the almost tangible gloom.

The big .50-caliber reaped another harvest of bone and flesh. A rearward squadsman picked out Bonner's position and gunned his bike, careening down the corridor of death at high speed, one hand guiding the bike, the other clutching an M3 grease gun. He fired as he went. Bonner saw him coming and imagined that the man saw himself as something of a hero.

The wire was two inches into his neck before the snowman realized what had happened.

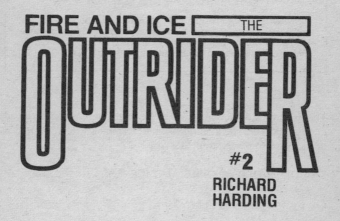

FIRE AND ICE THE

OUTRIDER

#2

RICHARD
HARDING

PINNACLE BOOKS   NEW YORK

This is a work of fiction. All the characters and events portrayed in this book are fictional, and any resemblance to real people or incidents is purely coincidental.

THE OUTRIDER #2: FIRE AND ICE

Copyright © 1984 by Robert Tine

An original Pinnacle Books edition, published for the first time anywhere.

First printing/August 1984

ISBN: 0-523-42213-X

Can. ISBN: 0-523-43205-4

Cover art by Michael Meritet

Printed in the United States of America

PINNACLE BOOKS, INC.
1430 Broadway
New York, New York 10018

9 8 7 6 5 4 3 2 1

FIRE AND ICE

Chapter One

Winter was coming on. Cold swept in from the north, cutting into Chicago, blowing icily through the broken streets. The city seemed to cower, like a captive before his captor, waiting for the great snows that would bury the city, wrapping the ruins in a cold white shroud. The snows were coming; they came every year, like an icy, victorious army driving its enemies before it. It was the worst time of the year in the lives of those who still lived on the continent that had once been called America, in the area once known as the United States.

Food would run short, fuel would be consumed too fast, and foraging for more would be difficult for the well-equipped raiders and smugglers and impossible for the poverty-stricken remainder of the population.

In the four feudal states that existed where America once stood proud, a lot of slaves would die that winter, while their jailers would rest warm and well fed through the season of ice, having enriched themselves at their slaves' expense.

In Chicago, as food ran out, men would reach for their guns and kill to get their share. And as winter wore on, the smugglers, raiders, road guides, pimps, whores—Chicago's diverse and violent population—would begin to quarrel. Living cheek by jowl, cooped up in the cold ruins, unable or unwilling to head out onto the ice-slick roads to do battle with the Stormers from the Slavestates or the Devils from the Hotstates, they would turn on each other. Dorca, the huge proprietor of a bar that carried his name, spent each night breaking up fights. He had a rule: no gunplay indoors. A lot of blood would stain the snow outside Dorca's.

The red flakes would stay there until covered by a fresh fall or the thaw came. . . .

Bonner was sure winter got longer each year. He lived in a few rooms on the old South Side, a tumble-down building he shared with the rats and the girl. Sometimes he looked up at the broken jagged remains of the old Chicago, the city that had been made up of buildings that tore into the sky. They amazed him. No one in the new world lived more than a few stories above the ground. The scared, the prudent, the powerless looked for shelter underground, where it was dark and cold, but safe, they thought. Bonner knew it didn't matter where you lived; no one was safe unless he handled a gun well and didn't hesitate to use it. Bonner was safe.

Bonner had chosen his little dwelling carefully. It was five rooms on the top floor of a four-story building. Each room in the ancient house was served by a fireplace, and set into the ceilings were cracked skylights showing a leaden cold sky. Thus Bonner could generate heat and he got as much of the daylight as he could. Throughout the new world light came from two main sources: the sun or kerosene lamps. But kerosene was hard to find so people resorted to smoky pitch torches. Houses were always burning down, and because there was no running water their owners could only watch them burn, flames consuming a man's whole store of food, clothing, ammunition—stuff that was almost impossible to replace. The very poor—the slaves—went to bed at nightfall.

There wasn't much furniture in Bonner's little flat. A bed, a few chairs—and books. They were stacked along the floor, jammed into gray metal shelves Bonner had found in a bombed-out office building in what had once been downtown. He collected books when he could, anything he could get his hands on. There was a vast blank spot, a wide dark unexplored sea in human learning, men on earth had no idea what had passed before them. No one really cared. Except Bonner.

Deep within him he felt the need to reclaim the past, hoping to find the key to his own time and to the future. It was painful work. References made by the ancient authors so casually meant nothing to him: Hitler, the Panama Canal, the Pope, Italy, a gas turbine, Albert Einstein, a nuclear reactor, a silicon chip, Vietnam. . . . Gradually, Bonner taught himself the rudiments of the past. Like a child taking his first clumsy steps, Bonner learned the old, dead facts. Some he understood completely, others he would never fathom. Hitler had been a world leader who had plunged the world into war—but it hadn't been he who destroyed the earth.

Bonner knew he was destined to fail, that ultimately he would be frustrated. There was a piece missing, nothing he read would ever tell him why the world had been bombed into ruins. The books always stopped short of explaining that; they never said what dredged up such hate in men that they wanted to kill an entire world. He learned that there had been another country called the USSR and that it was the natural enemy of the United States. These two countries were called superpowers and each was hell-bent on the destruction of the other.

Bonner presumed that they had started the war that had brought the world into a firestorm of death. But why? None of the books he read could explain that. He would never know why and it gnawed at him like a cancer. . . .

Bonner swung up off his bed and pulled on his heavy black boots. A fire burned in the grate in front of the bed. He tossed the book he had been reading— *Extraordinary Popular Delusions or the Madness of Crowds*—aside. The girl, a young woman who had attached herself to Bonner like a stray dog to a sympathetic kid, lay on the bed next to him. She watched his every move with jealousy.

''Are you going someplace?'' she asked.

''Dorca's.''

She sighed in relief. Hardly a moment passed that she didn't worry that Bonner was going to walk out and not return for months. But he had been sticking close to home a lot recently. He had vanished for a while during the summer and returned exhausted, sad, and with the look of a man hunted and haunted by his memories, his hates.

''Please be careful.''

He smiled gently. ''Okay,'' he said.

She was a nice girl, with soft wide blue eyes and long brown hair that fell down her shoulders. After they made love she would breathe passionately in his ear, ''I love you. . . .''

But Bonner's world, the life he led, didn't permit love . . . not anymore. He had loved once, a woman called Dara, a woman he had killed with his own hands. Mercy, love, devotion had made him kill her.

Many of the writers he read spoke of God. Gradually, over a thousand pages, Bonner had taught himself who God was. The sense of God was at once comforting and disquieting. He asked God: why? Why was Dara tortured by Leatherman? Why had the mechanics of the world placed Bonner in a position to chose between saving the woman he loved through killing her and allowing her torturer to live?

The questions multiplied. Why was the world ruined by the maneuverings of the men that were supposed to know better? Why had the world become a place where Leather and Berger and Carey held sway over innocent people. God was supposed to have the answers. He was supposed to know. He was supposed to guide the balanced, gentle action of the earth. . . . So little made sense to Bonner. And he wondered about it all the time. No good. No answers. No satisfaction. No long-dead man writing from beyond the grave. But Dara spoke to him, she was always there, always driving him, always carrying him back to those terrible minutes when he killed her and failed to kill Leather.

Somehow, Dara's death had sucked the soul from him. His ordinary red blood had been replaced with the hot liquor of hate. He lived now only to avenge her, to kill Leather, to kill the people—be they Slavestaters, Hotstaters, Snowstaters—who had been her enemies. Bonner could feel the old Outrider impulses coming back to him, but no longer felt the gentle guidance they had provided in the old days. He wanted to be an Outrider again but this time he wanted to kill. He wore his hate like a medal, a talisman that protected him. Bonner was fast, he was lethal, he was deadly, he had become a killing machine, fueled by hate.

Chapter Two

He walked through Chicago's cold broken streets headed for Dorca's. Dorca's was the only bar in Chicago and it was run by an old bear of a smuggler who decided to settle down and set himself up in business. If you needed anything—a drink, a girl, some information—you got it at Dorca's.

A couple of street workers, the lowest form of life in Chicago, ducked into an alleyway as Bonner passed. A street worker was a common thief who would try to take you down in the dark streets. The street workers preyed on the weak, the dumb, and the new arrivals, those runaways from the states who hadn't yet learned the ropes in wide-open Chicago. They didn't mess with Bonner, the smart ones, anyway, though some had tried. They died. Bonner was lightly armed. He carried a Supermatic Citation .22. It took a ten-shot clip. Bonner's trademark weapons—his three, heavy, lethal throwing knives and his cutdown Winchester shotgun—had been lost on his raid into Leatherman's Slavestates.

The usual riot was going on at Dorca's. The long low room was jammed with the toughest men on the continent. Bonner knew them all and even trusted a few. A number of the patrons had women draped over their shoulders or hanging off their arms. Dorca was no whoremonger, but he didn't object to free-lancers in his bar.

"Hey Bonner," shouted out a slimy pimp named Corner.

Bonner nodded in his direction. Corner was always at Dorca's, and he always had a drink in his hand. He longed to be accepted by the elite, the real men of Chicago, men like Bonner and those men he numbered among his friends

"Hey, Bonner, lemme give ya a drink."

"Later, Corner."

"How about a girl? Hey Suzie, come over here and take care of the man." A slim blond girl detached herself from a knot of women who stood in a corner gossiping. She walked toward Bonner, putting all the allure she could muster into her stride.

He held up his hands. "No thanks, Suzie." Suzie stopped, put her hands on her hips, and looked hurt.

"Whatsamatta?" yelled Corner. "You don't want my booze, you don't want my broads. What do you want, you prick?" His face was red and he had lurched up from the table; his hangers-on, his pilot fish, tried to restrain him. "Lemme go," he said, twisting free. "Hey Bonner, I'm fucking talking to you."

Bonner looked wearily at Corner. "Let it ride, man."

Men had stopped drinking and were watching now. A confused plan was beginning to form in Corner's mind. If he killed Bonner, if he killed the best, then the rest of them would have to respect him. . . . It never occurred to him that there was a reason why Bonner was the best. . . . The raw alcohol Dorca sold made him courageous, powerful, and stupid beyond words.

Bonner sighed. "Why don't you sit down, Corner, finish your drink, and leave me alone?"

"Whatsamatta? Scared?" A low ripple of laughter ran around the room. Bonner? Scared of *Corner*? Corner's cheeks flushed red. "You sonofabitch," he screamed, and jumped at Bonner.

Bonner took a step back and Corner landed in a heap at his feet. Bonner placed his heavily shod foot on the man's neck, pinning him to the floor.

"Now," he said, his teeth clenched, "are you going to behave?"

"Outside, Bonner, outside. I'll take you outside," Corner screamed, and squirmed under Bonner's boot.

"Corner," said Dorca, "if you go outside with Bonner, only Bonner is coming back in here. You'll get your ass handed to you."

"The hell I will," spat Corner.

"You're a good customer," said Dorca, "and I'd hate to lose you." He lumbered over to the prone pimp. Clutched in a hairy right paw was the instrument Dorca used to rule his establishment. It was the leg of an old pool table, elaborately carved and weighing about half a ton, but Dorca wielded it like a conductor's baton.

He picked Corner up by the scruff of the neck. Corner wriggled free and whipped a huge Super Comanche .44 Magnum from his belt. Dorca clubbed the gun out of his hand, then slapped the table leg onto Corner's jaw. He went out like a snuffed candle, and every man in the room winced at the sound of his teeth cracking.

"Get him out of here," Dorca bellowed at Corner's men. They dragged their boss out and everybody went back to drinking.

"What a dumb little shit," said Dorca, assuming his customary place at the end of the bar. In front of him, where other men would have had a drink, Dorca had a tall widemouthed jar filled with white sugar. He tipped it to his lips and took a swig. Dorca was a sugar freak and he knew all there was to know about the candy of the old days. A few of the candy wrappers from the past were kept framed behind the bar. Bonner made a point of giving any sweet thing he found to Dorca, a generosity that always moved Dorca to tears.

"You shoulda killed him," said Starling. Starling was Bonner's right-hand man. Together they had raided Leather and the Slavestates, dealing death as they moved through every mile in enemy territory.

"Waste of time," said Bonner.

"So what brings you in, Bonner," said Dorca, swigging back his sugar.

"Got tired of reading."

"Still hitting them books, huh?"

"Yep."

"Doing you any good?"

"Nope." Bonner smiled.

"Awwwww," said Starling, "that ain't true. He don't mean that. When we went to New York, he knew all about it."

"Hey Bonner," said Dorca, "you heard that the Slavestates are right in the middle of a gas drought. Any chance you had anything to do with that?" He smiled broadly. Every rider on the continent knew that Bonner had blown up the fuel reserves of the Slavestates.

"Hell," said Bonner, "I never went near the place. Blame that man there, Starling and his pal Harvey."

"Hows about we just blame Harvey?" laughed Starling. Harvey had not made it back from the mission. His scrawny body had been consumed in the huge fire he had set himself.

"Poor Harvey," said Dorca.

"Yeah, but he went out happy," said Starling.

"Seriously," said Dorca, "you hurt Leather bad. Riders coming in from the east say he's got patrols everywhere looking for gas. With winter coming on, they're going to need it bad."

"I'm sorry to have inconvenienced them," said Bonner.

Dorca threw his head back and rocked with laughter. As he did so, he saw the door of the joint open and standing there were Corner and his two thugs, all three with guns in their hands. They hunched their shoulders and threw out their arms in front of them in the classic combat stance.

Bonner saw them too. The .22 leaped into his hands as if it was alive. Corner's first shot shattered Dorca's jar of sugar. Bonner fired and a murderous .22 steel slug slapped, hot and true, into Corner's forehead. A red hole opened there, as if Corner had developed a third, bloodshot eye. Corner lived for less than half a second after impact. The bullet tore through his head and exited, depositing a piece of his brain—which had not served him well during his brief, violent life—on the door behind him.

Every other gun in the bar fired in what seemed like unison. Every shotgun, every revolver, every automatic, every rifle, even every dainty handgun carried by the whores fired after Bonner. Corner's two assistants were perforated from every angle by every type of shot and bullet. The wave of steel broke over them, tearing their flesh to brilliant scarlet tatters. Blood seemed to explode from them as if they were barrels. Bullets peppered around them, tearing up the floor at their feet and smashing the wooden doorframe.

As the chatter of gunfire died away, there was a moment of confused silence. No one could quite believe that Corner had come back and tried something so stupid.

A raider, still cradling his smoking shotgun said, "Hey, Dorca, anybody every try to take this place down before."

"Nope."

"Well, I reckon it's going to be awhile before anyone tries again." Laughter rolled around the room.

"Give 'em all a drink, Artie," ordered Dorca. His barman nodded and started setting up glasses.

Dorca turned to Bonner. "How do you like that guy Corner? What a jerk. Gonna miss his money, though. Say, you're pretty fast with that thing. The rest of the joint was a day and a half behind you."

"I broke the rule," said Bonner, "about shooting indoors."

"Yeah," said Dorca, laughing, "and am *I* pissed."

Chapter Three

Bonner tensed as soon as he heard the street door of his building open. Four stories below him he heard the heavy steps of two men. One of them mumbled to the other as they started up the stairs. As they did so, he picked up the girl's worn old shotgun and held it before him.

A voice from the stairs: "Hey Bonner, man, chill out, it's us . . ."

Bonner relaxed. The girl looked at him quizzically. "Who?"

"Seth and Starling."

She jumped out of bed and sprinted for another room. Bonner saw a quick glimpse of her long white legs, like a retreating deer. He swung out of bed and pulled on a pair of pants and a soft denim shirt. He was hauling on his boots when Seth and Starling arrived at the door.

"You're up early," said Bonner.

"We got plans, man." Seth was a black man about the size of Bonner, a couple of inches over six feet. He had the same powerful frame but was a little more developed. He had colossal biceps, and his chest, belly, and legs were tight with muscles. Other riders drove cars, Seth used a locomotive, a fiery contraption he ran himself, single-handed, doing the driving and the stoking of the hell-hot coal furnace. It was the kind of activity that made a man more than just strong; it filled him with an almost limitless reserve of force and will. He knew the rails the way Bonner knew the roads. Seth knew which lines were still passable, which switches still worked, which bridges still stood.

"Plans?" Bonner had heard that before. Plans always meant several thousand miles and several thousand rounds of ammunition, as well as a lot of blood, pain, and death. The riders always had plans. Bonner had even had a few himself over the years.

"And we think you might be interested," said Starling.

"Tell me about it."

"Okay," said Starling, "remember our last time out?"

"I'm not likely to forget it."

"Yeah." Starling's eyes glittered. "Remember how we picked up Cooker just inside the Slavestates, inside the Borderlands? Right after Trash Alley . . ."

"Yes, I remember." Cooker was a cranky, ornery gas hound. He was one of a few of a hardy breed, the gas hounds, the tank men, a group of men who looked for gasoline the way the old prospectors searched for gold. They rode old, homemade tank trucks, filling them where they could, then bringing the stuff back to Chi and selling it at exorbitant prices. Cooker had been the most driven, the most single-minded of the gas hounds. Starling and Bonner had rescued him from a Stormer patrol the last time out.

"Do you remember what he was babbling about when we found him?"

"He said he had found a gas tank farm."

"Yeah," said Starling enthusiastically, "what was it he called it?"

"The promised land," said Bonner.

"That's right! The promised land."

"Well," said Seth softly, "we want to go keep the promise. We want to find the tank farm."

"Be my guest," said Bonner.

"Yeah, now look Bonner, we want you to come along."

"Why?"

Seth laughed. "Bonner, we already know that there are Stormers rampaging out there. No one brings down Stormers better than you."

"I think you guys can handle it."

Through the thin door the girl, listening to the men converse, relaxed and closed her eyes as if giving thanks. Bonner didn't sound like he was going. Good, she thought, keep him here, with her, safe. . . .

"It would be a big help if you came along," said Starling. "Come on, what else you got to do?"

Bonner gestured around the book-strewn room. "I'm trying to catch up on my reading. I've got plenty to do."

"I know you, Bonner," laughed Seth. "There's only so much quiet you can take."

"Chi is never quiet."

"You know what I mean."

"Bonner," said Starling, "think of it, we could really score big on this one. Cooker wasn't kidding. It's out there, the gas, all you have to do is find it. No one knows the roads better than you. Man you could be rich."

Bonner shrugged. Seth spoke: "That's the wrong tactic, Starling. You know the man don't really care about money."

"We need you," said Starling simply.

On the other side of the door, the girl screwed her fists together tightly. Leave him alone, she wanted to scream, leave him here with me. She was worried. Bonner could never resist a call on his friendship. He had few friends, but those he had he was loyal to. If someone killed a friend, then Bonner killed his killer. It was that simple.

"You know the roads, Bonner, better than anyone."

"No," said Bonner, "there's someone a little better."

Seth and Starling looked puzzled. "Who?"

"Leather."

"Yeah, and he's probably out there right now looking for *our* gas."

Seth seized on this. Here was the tactic that would get Bonner to go along. "Yeah. You never know, Leatherman himself might be out there. In the open. You could take him, Bonner. This time you could get him."

The faintest sign of pain flitted across Bonner's hard features, as if Seth had found a bruise on his lean body and had pressed on it. "Leather won't leave the Cap."

"He'd leave Washington if he had to. If he knows the roads better than anyone, even you, it would seem plain to me that he would be the one to lead the expedition."

"Look, Seth, you know what we did to him, I mean him personally, when we were in the Cap."

"Yeah."

"I cut off his hands. . . ." Bonner held his own out in front of him. "What is he going to do on the road without any hands?"

"He'll be protected," said Starling.

"Sure," said Bonner, "but Leather has to have a gun in his hands to feel like a man. He won't show himself outside the Cap."

"You know the man," conceded Seth, "but if

things got that bad, if only he could lead the Stormers, then he would have to go. Man, the Slavestates run on gas. If he can't get any, he's a dead man.''

Bonner looked at him. Seth and Starling could see Bonner's blue eyes provide his own silent extension of that statement. Leather was a dead man already. One day Bonner would get him, and kill him. The jury had returned its verdict, the judge had pronounced his sentence: Leatherman would die, Bonner would be his executioner.

Seth's voice was husky. "He's out there man, he's out there. . . ."

"And you could take him," said Starling, leaning forward.

A thousand different thoughts raced through Bonner's mind, each a good, balanced thought: he wondered about the number of people Leather would have with him, he wondered if Leather would ever allow himself to leave his power base, he wondered if the three of them could ever find Leather in that vast shattered continent, he wondered about the odds. . . . But all of that was washed away in a single blood-red tide of hate. Leather must die. Bonner must kill him.

Bonner exhaled heavily. "Okay guys, you just bought youself an old Outrider."

"Good," said Seth, smiling broadly.

"Awwwwwright," said Starling.

Behind the door the girl laid her head against the wooden frame and felt hot tears flow into her eyes.

One day he would leave and he wouldn't come back. She cursed Starling and she cursed Seth, and deep down inside her, somewhere in the center of her love for him, she cursed Bonner and his burning sense of duty and revenge.

Chapter Four

As soon as Bonner decided to go, he swung into action. There were preparations to be made. The key to any successful ride—and a successful ride was one where the rider came back alive, whole, or at least, without having lost too much blood—was proper preparation. Bonner was always amazed that people inbound for hostile territory would take along a rusty old Marlin rifle, half a tank of gas, and a great deal of faith that they were meaner, tougher, and faster than any man they were likely to meet. Sometimes these guys came back. They would spend a week or two in Chi getting blitzed at Dorca's, then they went out again. Bonner had seen them come into town and a couple of times had been present when they went—permanently.

Life was hard, thought Bonner, but it was much harder if you were stupid.

There were two important struts that supported a rider on the road, two granite blocks that were the foundation of any man when he went out to do battle. He had to have a reliable means of transport and he had to have a weapon he could always depend on. The right gun had to fit a man like his skin and he had to be able to use it as if it was an extension of himself. It had to be as flexible as a whip, yet as hard and as strong as a well-worked-out muscle.

Bonner was a master of the knife. Time was when three heavy, razor-sharp knives hung from a holster on his hip. They were ready to fly through the air with unerring accuracy. They would cut deep into the bodies of his enemies, silver, fine-edged extensions of his own power. The steel would snap through the flesh, the gristly muscle, the soft pliant veins and arteries, of those unlucky enough to have tried to take Bonner down.

He backed up his blades with a shotgun, 12-gauge, two barrels, instant death. Bonner could whip his gun from its nest and lay down a carpet of fire that devastated all those who opposed his will.

But Bonner had suffered a setback, a humiliation. On the last raid into the Slavestates he had lost his weapons. Leather had them now. Bonner could get new ones, a gun and a set of knives that men might even consider better than his old ones, but he could never replace the ones he had lost.

But replacements had to be found. Bonner never cut corners on his arms. He wanted the best and he didn't care what he paid. He could have gone to the bazaar, that teeming, noisy, cramped shopping center on the Loop, and buy alongside all the other raiders, smugglers, and riders that were looking for weaponry. But Bonner was prepared to pay top slate for his weaponry. Cut corners there and you were cutting your own throat. Bonner went to the Armorer.

The Armorer had a shop over on the South Side and his four or five dark rooms were filled with weapons of every variety. He rarely left his lair. The Armorer would not sell to just anyone. He had to be sure you would take care of his babies and he had to be sure that you knew how to use them, appreciate them like a connoisseur.

"Why should I bust my ass," he would growl, "to sell to some pile of meat whose only qualification for my stuff is that he can pay for it?" He would harumph indignantly. "Any fuck can get hold of money."

Bonner saw in the Armorer an embodiment of a certain type of man the ancient authors had written about with much respect: an artist. If there was such a thing as an artist in this new, deadly age, the Armorer was it. Bonner recognized that what the Armorer could do with tubes of steel, pieces of wood, and tiny wasps packed with gunpowder and lead was as important to that day as what the great artists of the past had done to theirs. The Armorer worked within his medium to create those things that would destroy in the cause of good, or at least, work to the advantage of those men who were not as bad as most. Men like the Armorer, Bonner, Seth, and Starling sensed that things were badly out of kilter in the world, that everyone was guilty of crimes, but that some were guiltier than others.

Bonner rapped smartly on the Armorer's door. His knock rang in the silence. From the other side of the door there was nothing but quiet. Bonner knocked again. A heavy, even tread advanced toward the door.

"Who?" demanded a voice from within.

"Bonner."

A lock was snapped, a bolt shot back.

"Bonner," said the Armorer, swinging the door open. He spoke through a dense mat of black beard streaked with gray. "What brings you to me?"

"I need some weapons."

The Armorer was a tall man and always wore a long, lose robe; he looked like the pictures of the Old Testament prophets that Bonner had seen in his books. He must have weighed three hundred pounds and his forearms glistened as if they had been oiled. He spent long hours at his anvil, hammer in hand, and he had arms as strong and as hard as tree limbs.

His vast face darkened. "So what happened to your old stuff?"

"I lost it," Bonner said simply.

The huge oaken door slammed in his face. Bonner

looked at the door and smiled. He knocked again. Time passed. Then, from the other side, the Armorer spoke.

"Go away."

"Come on," said Bonner.

"Why should I fit you again? You're only going to lose the stuff I present to you."

As far as the Armorer was concerned, he never sold you anything. He loaned it to you. It was always his, and if you lost it, misused it, or destroyed it, he considered it as serious as if you had hurt one of his children.

"Armorer," said Bonner, "I need help."

A bolt was shot back and the door swung open.

"You're lucky I like you," he said. "Get in here."

The room smelled of woodsmoke and hot metal. Bits and pieces of a thousand different weapons littered the weighty oak tables. The forge glowed dully, heating the room.

"Take a seat," said the Armorer. Bonner settled himself in a chair and the Armorer sat across from him and leaned on the table. "Now," he said, "before we talk about your new stuff, suppose we have a little chat about what happened to your old stuff."

As quickly as he could, Bonner recapped his long, long, bloody strike deep into the dark gut of Leatherman's empire. He spoke flatly, telling the Armorer only the details he needed to know. Bonner wasn't big on war stories. He finished by telling him that Leather now held the weapons.

"And he's probably slicing the shit out of his slaves right now," said the Armorer.

"No," said Bonner firmly, "he's not."

"How do you know?"

"He has no hands," said Bonner matter-of-factly.

The Armorer looked puzzled. Bonner wasn't the type that went in for mutilations.

Bonner seemed to read his thoughts. "It was an accident," he said.

"You *accidentally* cut off his hands?"

"I was trying to kill him."

"What did you use to bring him down?"

"An ax."

"Oh."

Bonner said nothing about the circumstances of Dara's death. That he had not been able to save her was a shame he would never allow himself to forget. Nor would he be able to forgive himself so grotesque a failure.

"Tough time all over, sounds like," said the Armorer sympathetically. He sat back in his rickety chair. "So what do you need?"

"Knives, shotgun . . . some ammunition."

"Yeah, I can fix you up." The Armorer stood heavily.

"Have you ever heard of a gun called a Steyr AUG?" asked Bonner.

"I got a book that lists it. Never seen one. You have one?"

"Yes. Picked it up in New York."

"How is it?"

"Semi-automatic, fast, tough, ugly."

"Sounds good."

"Do you have any ammunition that'll fit it?"

"You making a change, Bonner? You never carried an automatic before."

"It came in handy."

The Armorer's eyes narrowed. "You headed out again?"

Bonner's mouth set in a hard line. "Yes, guess so."

"Yeah," said the Armorer, "I got some ammo that should help you out some."

"Good."

"Shotgun first." The Armorer rooted around in the metal mess and tangle that littered the rooms. He came up with the object of his search a moment later, a long slim bundle wrapped in an old gray blanket. The Armorer slipped the gun out from its covering, his eyes bright with admiration.

"Nice," said Bonner.

"Purdy Special," said the Armorer. "They're old, very old, but its the finest work I've ever seen. Back then, Bonner, in the old days, they knew how to do things."

Bonner took the gun in his hands. It was a long, slim, elegant piece of work, and somehow it reminded him of the body of the girl. He could feel the balance of the gun in his hands, and as he ran his fingers over the butter-smooth stock and barrels he

could sense the sure hand of the long-dead craftsman
who had fashioned it.

"Can you cut it down?"

A look of intense pain dashed across the Armorer's
face. "Yeah, I can," he said, "but it won't be the
same gun."

"I know," said Bonner bluntly. He couldn't allow
himself to worry about besmirching this thing of
beauty. He needed the firepower.

"Knives," said the Armorer, producing three flat-
bladed, razor-sharp blades, the identical counterparts
of Bonner's old ones. They had the same weight, the
same black bone handles, the same cold assuredness
of purpose as the knives that Leather now had.

The Armorer found ammunition to fit the shotgun,
the Steyr, and even threw in a belt or two of the
ammunition that would fit the heavy machine gun
that Bonner had mounted on his car.

"What do I have to pay you."

"A thousand slates," said the Armorer. The price
was high but fair. Bonner was not the sort of man
who would haggle. The Armorer wasn't the sort of
man who would cheat him. Bonner paid in the cur-
rency of the day: odd pieces of gold and silver that
had been melted down and restamped into rough,
round wafers.

The money lay glittering on the table, but the
Armorer paid very little attention to it. His large
brown eyes were fixed on Bonner. "Do me a favor,"
he said, "try and get your old stuff back from
Leatherman."

"Will do," said Bonner.

"And be careful about it," added the Armorer, knowing that would be impossible for the Outrider.

Chapter Five

The bus station building housed Lucky, and Lucky was the best mechanic in Chicago. He was a stunted, pale little man with a shattered kneecap that made his leg stick out to one side. He walked awkwardly, dragging his leg behind him. Between his extremely pale coloring and his odd crabbed walk, he looked like some sort of peculiar creature that had grown used to being underground. The duty of looking after Bonner's car fell to Lucky.

"No finer machine on the continent," he would say proudly. The car was an exquisite creation, all of it the work of Lucky. Lucky was to engines what the Armorer was to weapons.

The car stood in an old bus bay, and it looked tense, anxious, as it seemed to set its fat, smooth tires down onto the broken, prebomb roads.

The vehicle was mostly engine. The area from front axle to steering column was taken up by a long, rectangular straight-eight Lycoming marine engine. Lucky had salvaged it from the rotting hulk of a speedboat he found on the bed of what had once been Lake Michigan. The big block of engine looked like a coffin nestled in a rat's nest of electrical cable and cooling hoses.

The big engine was mounted on an all-pipe chassis that Lucky had assembled on his own, double welding the heavy metal together to make sure it would support the combined weight of the heavy engine and the mammoth fuel tank. Gas was hard to find everywhere but it was harder to find on the road than anywhere else, and every rider tried to carry enough to see him through his journey. But it was always a trade-off: the more gas you carried the more weight you carried, and the more weight you carried the more gas you had to burn to carry it. Lucky had done some rudimentary calculations and decided that Bonner could carry fifty gals no problem.

A graceful rollbar swept over the driver's head, a hard metal arch that would protect Bonner if he should ever have the ill luck to actually tip his vehicle over.

Mounted on that bar was a .50-caliber machine gun, a piece of heavy artillery that Bonner could use like a pro and which had gotten him out of a jam more than once.

"She's the fastest, she's the meanest, she's the toughest, the best little machine riding the roads today,'' boasted Lucky, ''and you still treat her like shit,'' he finished disgustedly.

"The lady and I have an understanding,'' said Bonner with a smile. Lucky was always giving Bonner hell about his mistreatment of the iron warhorse.

"Yeah? What understanding?'' Like the Armorer, Lucky was sure that no one could ever understand his art the way he did. The cars were always his babies and mistreating them was a sin of the gravest kind. Of course, again like the Armorer, there was probably no sin that Lucky couldn't forgive Bonner, the man he always called the boss.

"She takes me where I want to go,'' said Bonner, ''and I promise that I'll return her to her daddy Lucky.''

"Good thing too,'' said Lucky.

Bonner slid behind the wheel and hit the starter. The big engine boomed into life. Lucky smiled happily. The blast of that powerful engine, the throaty roar from its twin exhaust pipes, was the sweetest music in the world to him. He could have listened to it for hours without tiring of it.

Bonner slid the car into gear, but before he could take off, Lucky shouted a question: "Where you going?''

"Slavestates.''

"Again? What for?''

Bonner thought about that for a second. He was going, not for gas, not for poor dead Cooker's promised land, he was going to find Leather and his evil

forces and this time . . . this time . . . "Gas," he
said.

"Good," said Lucky, "there's not a hell of a lot
of the stuff around these days."

Bonner tossed a wave in the direction of the little
mechanic and then hit the gas, screaming down the
ramp. The loud exhaust from the twin pipes just
behind Bonner's shoulders blared their internal-
combustion life into the enclosed space.

The car and driver burst out into the daylight.
Waiting at the base of the ramp was Starling. He was
mounted on a huge red panhead Harley Davidson, a
piece of loot he had won from a fearful squad of
Radleps that he and Bonner had encountered and
destroyed during their raid into the Slavestates. It
was a couple of yards of pure power and obviously
had once been the prized possession of some long-
forgotten biker who had eaten up the miles on his
proud steed.

Standing next to the hard, wiry rider were two
men, their giant forms casting long shadows in the
morning sun.

Bonner stopped short, the screech of brakes sending shivers down the spine of Lucky, who watched
from the upper stories of the bus station.

"Watch them brakes, boss," shouted Lucky.

"Hey," said Bonner, smiling broadly, "the Mean
Brothers."

The Mean Brothers lumbered over to Bonner and
tried to crush him in a bear hug. "That's okay,
Means," said Bonner, "good to see you too."

The Brothers were identical twins, both great bears of men, each covered with hair matted like fur. They were mutes so no one knew their names, if indeed, they had names at all. Bonner had sprung them from a Leatherman prison on Prison Island in New York—he hadn't planned to, but that was the way things worked out—and now the Mean Brothers were his friends for life. You could see it in their eyes: they would never forget Bonner's kindness, they would never betray him, they would cheerfully die for him. They would follow him into the jaws of hell if he would lead them there. If you became the Mean Brothers' friend, they would never let you down. If you became their enemy, they would not rest until they brought you down.

The Mean Brothers' weapons were an ax and a shovel, the implements having been presents from Bonner. Prior to that they had been able to do a large amount of damage using only the great strength of their hands. Despite the chill they were clad in their usual clothing, shorts and leather sandals. It was as if they relied on their luxuriant body hair to keep them warm.

"I thought they might want to come along," said Starling. "You want to come along, Mean Brothers?"

The Mean Brothers nodded vigorously.

"See, they want to go. There must be a few Stormers left they ain't killed yet."

At the mention of the Stormers the Mean Brothers' huge faces darkened.

"I have a feeling they would hold it against us if we didn't take them with us," said Bonner.

"Yeah, and it would be our bringdown," said Starling.

One of the Mean Brothers shook his head vigorously. No, he was saying, it was Bonner's decision. They would never try to hurt him.

"Just kidding, Mean Brother," said Starling. "We was just having a little fun."

The Mean Brother shrugged as if to say: "Some joke."

"Think they'll be warm enough?" asked Bonner.

Starling slipped his scooter into gear. "Hey, they look worried to you?"

"No."

"They look sick to you?"

"Nope."

"Then?"

"Okay, Mean Brothers, let's go." The two giants jumped aboard, settling down on the big exposed fuel tank.

"Hit it, Starling," said Bonner.

The tall, thin, deadly rider gave the Outrider the thumbs-up and released his brake, bouncing down the cracked Chicago streets.

They navigated their way through what had once been downtown and swung out onto the once-fashionable and rich Lake Shore Drive. There they could see the rising morning sun sweeping gold and pink light out onto the brown, dead lake bed. There lay the main east-west road into Chicago. There was no other way in and the citizens of Chi liked it that way. No one would ever be able to bring a force of any size across the vast expanse of emptiness without being seen. That way the whole city avoided a sudden raid from the feudal states.

The Slaves, the Hots, the Snows hated Chicago. It was an open city, a place where men who refused to submit to the boot of another man found their refuge. If they had their way, the heads of the States would have wiped out the men of Chicago, but they knew that to take on Chicago meant losing most of their best men for little return. Chicago was the town that you went to if you thought you were tough enough to make it on your own, to live by your wits and your gun.

Once in a while a runaway slave from the feudal states would wander into Chicago. The feeling among those who lived in the city was that once you made it that far you deserved to live, so if Stormers or Devils or Lightnings came looking for you, every gun in Chi-town would be turned against your enemies. If a member of the town decided that he didn't like your face or your talk—well, that was personal, between you and him and may the toughest, or the dirtiest, fighter win.

Bonner and Starling's wheels hit the hard-packed lake bed and began to consume the miles voraciously. No one knew what happened to the lake. The bomb had removed it somehow. Bonner always thought he would loved to have seen that much water right there in the middle of the continent. It must have been an amazing sight. They pointed their noses for the east and Bonner couldn't suppress the strength of the joy he felt. He wanted another shot at Leather, he wanted to hit the road again, he wanted the activity, the nerve-tingling duel with death. He looked into the sun and felt the cold wind whip around his neck. It was the kind of day that demanded that a man get in his car and go—to see what was out there, to see how many more of his foes he could vanquish.

Seth's big steam locomotive eased out of the yards where the vast old Chicago station had stood. Acres upon acres of rusting rails glistened in the morning sun, blood red where the icy rays of the sun hit the centuries-old corrosion. He stood on the foot plate and peered ahead of him. There were numerous switches on the line that he had to throw before he could make his way out of the Chicago yards. He worked his mind over them as if he was solving a giant complex puzzle.

He set the train on a slow throttle and then jumped down from the engine. He raced a few paces ahead of the slow-moving behemoth, grabbed the heavy weighted lever of the switch, and threw it effortlessly. He stood by the side of the rail and waited for his train to catch up with him, like a dutiful pet. He stepped lightly onto the vehicle and tugged on the throttle. The engine picked up speed and curved over the track he had set for it. Behind him stood the giant coal car that he filled himself in the dangerous, hateful firelands. The firelands were Seth's domain. . . .

Behind the coal car were three tanker cars that he had coupled onto his engine the night before. They would be the first carriers of the gas out of the promised land. It wasn't much, but it was more gas than Chicago had seen around in one place in a long time.

Seth pushed the throttle up a bit more and the train picked up more speed. He jumped down from the cab again and swung another switch open.

"East," he said aloud, as he jumped back onto the foot plate. He felt Bonner's sense of elation. A crisp morning, the open rails, a mission, an adventure, a prize . . . He clutched his little M3 machine gun—it was always slung over his shoulder—to his side and did a little dance on the foot plate.

"East," he said again, happy, and yanked on the whistle. The long, ghostly howl echoed out over the railyards and beyond, into the sleeping broken city.

=====================Chapter Six

That low blast from Seth's train whistle rolled across the city like smoke gently bouncing off the broken walls of a thousand dead buildings and awoke two people.

The girl opened her eyes in the empty apartment and looked at the bright sunlight passing through the cracked windows of the skylight. Tears flowed from her eyes onto the pillow and she felt the place in the bed where her man's body had lain an hour before. Gone again, she thought. Would this be the time he wouldn't return. She drove the thought from her mind and cheered herself up with a single thought: Bonner was the Outrider, and the Outrider didn't fall.

*   *   *

Savage snorted in his sleep and the snort awakened him. A second blast from the whistle pulled him to full awareness.

"Whassat?" he said aloud.

He swung out of bed and wandered into another room. Spread out on the floor, in a tangle of blankets and sheets, lay Savage's lieutenant, one of the big raider's best riders. Savage led the largest group of raiders in Chicago. He had under his command a force of about forty men with guns and bikes, and Savage made sure that his crew lived up to their leader's name. Most men felt that Savage's raiders were no better than Stormers.

Savage kicked the man awake. "What?" said the man.

"Franklin," ordered Savage, "get up."

"Wha'for?"

"Cause I want to talk to you."

"Jeez, boss."

Savage kicked him again. "Get up when I tell you to."

Franklin hiked himself up on his thin elbows. "Okay, okay, I'm all ears." He could feel the unwelcome morning aftereffects of a night at Dorca's swirling around his brain.

"I heard that crazy nigger's whistle blow."

Franklin looked at Savage as if he was crazy. "You woke me up to tell me that?" Was Savage finally losing it, he wondered.

"Don't sass me, Franklin," said Savage threateningly.

Franklin thought a moment and figured that the boss was probably giving him some pretty good advice. "Sorry, boss."

"That's better. So where's he going?"

"Seth? He's inbound for who knows where, him, Starling, Bonner."

"I thought Bonner didn't ride this time of year."

"So this time he is," said Franklin patiently. "You know what Bonner's like. He makes his own rules."

"He's riding with Starling, right?"

"Yeah."

"And he has Seth tailing him in that thing of his?"

"Yeah."

"Then it's big."

Bonner never did anything small, thought Franklin. He hoped that the boss wasn't thinking of going after them. Franklin just wasn't in the mood for a firefight in the cold—though a firefight with Bonner would certainly warm things up in a hurry. Franklin was settled in for the winter.

Franklin thumped the pillow, as if he was about to lie down again. "How can you be sure its so big?"

Savage kicked the pillow out from beneath his subordinate's head. "Because I'm smart. Round up the riders."

"Awwww, boss . . ."

It took awhile to round up Savage's band from the lodgings and brothels in the ruined city; most were, like Franklin, nursing heavyweight hangovers, and the loud rumbling of the two-score bikes and cars hurt a lot of heads. Street workers watched the force assemble from the shadows and wondered where the hell Savage and his crew were headed. The raiding season was just about over. Anything of value in the feudal states had already been shipped to the various capitals.

Like a single, many-headed steel beast the raiders hit the road, thundering down on the lake bed and heading east.

Savage was on the lead bike. He figured that Bonner and Starling had a few hours on them. No problem, he thought. He just wanted to get close enough to follow them a ways, to find out what was so big that it brought Starling and Bonner out onto the road so late in the season. It had to be a hell of a prize and Savage wanted it, whatever it was.

Savage held up his hand and the two riders just behind him moved up alongside him. One was Franklin.

"Frankie," bellowed Savage, "slow the boys down a little. I don't want Bonner to hear so many bikes on his ass."

Franklin nodded. "Check," he said, and drifted back to slow the column down.

Savage turned to the man on his left. "Scotty, I want you to take four or five men out and scout out ahead of us. Take off man, catch up with Bonner. Keep him in sight, keep him close, but don't try to take him. When you got him, send one of the boys back. Got it?"

The man nodded.

"Then hit it."

Five bikes and a man mounted on a cycle/sidecar combination took off ahead of the column. In a matter of seconds, they were just dots on the horizon. Savage settled back in the padded saddle of his bike. He congratulated himself. He was a smart man.

The main force rode on another hour, throwing up a huge column of dust from the brown lake bed. Then they started seeing trouble signs. Suddenly, up ahead on the horizon, Savage saw a lump, something spread out on the ground. Smoke seemed to rise from it.

The raider force closed on it and when they were a couple of hundred yards from their target they could see that it was one of their scouts. His body—what was left of it—lay next to his burning bike. Flame had danced from the exploded fuel tank over the chassis of the bike, scorching the paint and catching the tires, which belched black, acrid smoke into the clear blue sky.

The scout's shattered body was sprawled on the lake bed. The upper half of his torso seemed to have disappeared. Bits and pieces of the man were scattered in a wide bloody circle around him. The man's waist and legs were still a single unit, and entrails spilled out from the top of his pants like the stuffing from an old sofa.

"Stupid motherfuckers," said Savage. "I told them not to try and take the man down."

Franklin looked out toward the horizon, following the tire tracks with his eyes. "They went after him."

"Then they are dead men."

"Hey Savage," called out one of the raiders, "who fucked Mickey so bad."

"Starling," said Savage, "and those lousy arrows of his." He gave the signal and the column moved out.

At various points along the road they found more bloody milestones. A couple of the raiders had been blown to pieces like their brother on the road behind them. A couple had been shot—big divots of flesh had been chewed out of their bodies by the sharp bite of Bonner's .50-caliber.

"How many is that?"

"Five," said Franklin.

"You don't think Whiskey would be stupid enough to try and take them hisself?"

"No one is that dumb."

The column moved on, expecting at any moment to find the bloody remains of Whiskey on the road. Then they saw on the road ahead of them a bike, still standing, bumping down the track toward them. It was coming on very slowly.

"That's Whiskey," said Franklin.

"He's been hit," said Savage. The raider was slumped over the handlebars of his bike, moving toward them very slowly. The column met the broken biker and saw that blood seemed to drip from him like dew. His face was flat against the big headlight and the only reason the bike stayed erect was because it was a three-wheeler. If he had been riding a two-wheeled machine, he never would have made it. A raider jumped from his own steed and grabbed the handbrake on the crossbar and stopped the bike just in front of Savage.

''Another one dead,'' said Savage.

The raider that had stopped the bike reached down to kill the engine. Just as he bent over, Savage noticed that the handlebars had been tied together and jammed so that the bike would point back along the road. Whiskey hadn't done that, Savage thought, Bonner had.

''Wait,'' he shouted.

But it was too late. As soon as the raider turned off the big engine, the connection was made. The bike, layered with explosives, detonated. The boom was deafening and the parts of the bike blown asunder by the force of the blast scythed through the mingling raiders with a ferocious flash of death. The raider who had stopped the bike vanished in a metal storm of forks and spokes. The next-closest person to the death machine was poor Savage. . . . A piece of the old Harley's frame caught him mid-gut and he doubled over it, as if trying to stop the twisted metal from burrowing into his big body. The pain of the cut tore an impassioned scream from his throat.

A dozen other raiders went down when the bike went up. Some were killed instantly, others lay groaning on the packed cold earth, their staring shocked eyes watching as their lifeblood pumped out onto the hungry dirt.

Franklin was spared. He couldn't believe his good fortune. Around him lay the dead or dying members of Savage's once-proud force. Those still alive, perhaps twenty of them, couldn't believe that their numbers had been taken apart without even having seen the enemy.

They looked to Franklin as the new leader. "So what the fuck do we do now?" asked one raider.

Franklin wiped his hand through his hair. The boss was dead and half—more than half—his force was gone.

"I say fuck it," said Franklin. "Let's go home."

"Good idea," said one of the raiders. They slowly turned around and left their dead for the snows and the cold. They headed back to Chi with Franklin leading the way. He wondered if the boss had even thought of the chance of his getting killed when he kicked Franklin awake that morning. Probably not. But now he was dead. Stupid fuck.

"I knew this was a bad idea," said Franklin into the wind.

════════════════════Chapter Seven

Riders called it Trash Alley. It was a former super-
highway jammed with the rusting ruins of thousands
of old automobiles. Every lane of the old dead roadway was packed with cars, all of them, in every lane,
facing in the same direction: west.

Bonner figured they must have been running away.
Running away from a war that had somehow started
in the east and was sweeping west. The scared citi-
zenry had taken to the road, and in their panic they
had trapped themselves there on the highway, a highway that ran nowhere, except to death.

Trash Alley was tough passage for Bonner, Starling,
and the other riders that dared to go into the Slavestates,
but it was the path they took because it was just
about the only way in. South of them lay the firelands,

the burning border of the Slavestates. The firelands were a continuous belt of fire that shielded most of the Slavers' western flank from attack. A few men, Bonner among them, knew their way through the firelands, but no one, not even Bonner, traveled willingly through that burning flame swamp—except Seth. He reveled in the smoky fire pits, traveling through them as easily as a rider on a wide-open stretch of desert highway in the Hotstates.

Bonner and Starling traveled slowly along the fifty dirty miles of the alley. They had to take it slow as they were guiding their vehicles between the rusty steel reefs that were the brokendown cars and trucks of drivers long dead. The alley always depressed Bonner, seeing in these decaying pieces of transport the whole scenario, the complete, violent picture of the death throes of the old world. Behind every wheel had been a panicked driver, a terrified family huddling by his side; a darkening sky, flat, unemotional instructions on the radio; incomprehension, disbelief, anger, fear turning to terror then giving way to mass hysteria.

Riding up swiftly behind them came terrible history, fate—the massive movements of mankind that would sweep these ordinary folks up into its grasp. Men who had once just worked and ate and slept and cast a bored eye on the events of the day at work's end were suddenly part of them. They were there on the road because of men and policies far away from their tiny lives. The distant events of history swept over them, suddenly, painfully. Death.

Starling was in the lead and keeping his head down. Stormers patrolled Trash Alley—they patrolled all of the Borderlands. When they couldn't be there in person, they left some very unpleasant calling cards: wire traps that would slice easily through a man's neck, explosive traps, powerful mines that were tripped by your front wheels but didn't explode until the middle of the vehicle, where the driver sat, passed overhead; spring guns that would blast a couple of pounds of shot into the rusty canyon, nail traps, gas traps, glass traps. Some of the Stormers could be quite resourceful when they turned their nasty little minds to it.

Starling moved cautiously. He was a veteran of a hundred rides through Trash Alley and he was an expert at spotting each different death nest that the Stormers had planted along the way. He was also expert at turning the traps against the men who had set them. Starling always carried a wire and wasn't above placing it where he knew a Stormer was likely to appear.

He started slowing down and Bonner tapped his brakes. Starling came to a complete stop in the narrow passage, the sound of the big pounding Harley engine bouncing off the high metal walls.

Starling swiveled in his seat and looked at Bonner. Bonner stared back. It was unlike Starling to stop in the alley for no reason.

"Bonner," called Starling over his shoulder, "there's something not right here."

Bonner stood up in the seat of his steel warhorse. "What's the problem?"

"That's the problem," said Starling. "There is no problem. There's nothing along here at all. Nothing. I'd swear that no Stormer patrol has been through here in days, weeks maybe. We passed two traps, a nail gun and a wire, and someone had taken them apart."

"A rider maybe," said Bonner.

"That's what I figured, but who? Everyone is back in Chi-town."

"Now we don't know that for a fact," said Bonner.

Starling settled back down on the big saddle and gunned his engine. "No," he said, "I s'pose."

But Bonner could see in the hunch of the rider's shoulders that he was puzzled and alert to the possibilities of danger. The Mean Brothers sat behind Bonner, seemingly unaware of the danger that worried Starling or the cold, which was getting worse with the passing of each minute.

Night was falling as they eased out of the alley unscathed. Starling and Bonner changed positions, Bonner sliding into the lead. Attached to the prow of his narrow coffin of a car was a heavy theatrical spotlight. It could cut a path in the darkness several hundred yards long.

It was not long after night came that the temperature plunged and the snow came, first in feathery little squalls, then in ever-deepening waves of whiteness. It danced in front of the blast of light and spun crazily into his face. Twice they had to stop to put on clothing enough to withstand the bad weather. Bonner was wearing his goggles and heavy gauntlets and the rough fur coat that covered him from head to foot. But he was still cold. The Mean Brothers blinked away the snow and looked with bemused disgust at the frailties of their fellowman—if the Mean Brothers could be considered men. They were really more like creatures trapped between floors on the elevator of evolution. They knew that eventually they would feel the cold, but the first snows of winter mattered to them not at all.

"How much farther you wanna go?" asked Starling. The snow was really picking up now, approaching the force of a blizzard.

"Head on until we get to the place where we found Cooker." The last time out they had found the poor old gas hound trussed up like a chicken in the forecourt of an old motel. He had been captured by Stormers and Bonner and Starling had set him free.

"You remember where it was?"

"Think so," said Bonner.

As they stole on through the cold white night they found themselves slowing down to a crawl. Bonner was driving on instinct and memory. Although they were out of Trash Alley, the road was littered with broken masonry and junked cars. Bonner had cut his light; it was worse than useless. He could still hardly see anything.

Coming up ahead he could just make out the line of one of the few overpasses on the old highway that still stood. As they approached it Bonner saw, unmistakably, the orange and blue flame of a muzzle flash. A force, a small one, but a force nonetheless was dug in on the bridge above him. Bonner hit the gas.

"Hold on, Meanies," he yelled, and the big car lurched forward, the fat tires thrumming on the cracked asphalt. The big twin exhaust pipes opened up and the sound cut through the snowy night. He heard Starling push his big bike right up behind him. Together, side by side, they tore a wide gash in the white curtain of snow.

A rip of bullets streamed by Bonner's ear and he shot a glance over his shoulder. The overpass was lost in a swirl of snow, but he could tell exactly where the bridge was. It was picked out by a line of muzzle flashes, spewing bullets into the whiteness.

Bonner was steering blind, hoping that there was no old junked bus or a slab of bridge pillar lying in the road ahead. The mixture of snow and blackness played havoc with his sense of distance. He hunched over the wheel, squinting into the icy darkness. Then, relaxed, he slumped back in his seat. If it was going to happen, it was going to happen. He decided to worry about something he could do something about: the unknown men behind him who were definitely trying to kill him. That much he was sure of.

A bumpy, black five miles passed in a matter of seconds. Bonner hit the brakes. Starling glided up next to him.

"Who the fuck was that?" screamed Starling. Snow

was matted on his leather jacket and in between the fingers of his gauntlets.

"Good question," said Bonner. "Shut down." They killed their engines and suddenly the night was quiet save for the low moan of the wind and the snow hissing on the hot engines. Bonner sat stock still, like a beast of prey sensing his quarry.

Through the night it came, like the howl of a wolf. A dark, cold chorus of engines . . .

"Seven," said Starling.

"Yeah," said Bonner, "bikes."

In the snow-wrapped night they saw the first probings of powerful spots.

"Who?" said Starling.

"No idea, but they're not very friendly."

"Stand or go?"

"Do you feel like chasing all over the place tonight."

"Nope."

"Me neither. Stand."

The sky behind the riders was lighting up as the headlights of their pursuers refracted off the swirling snow.

Bonner muscled his car up onto the shoulder of the highway. When the lights hit that part of the road he didn't want to be sitting there giving them any kind of target.

The two men moved quickly. Starling too had moved to the side of the road and carefully put his bike under the cover of a slab of pavement. Then he

readied himself to do battle with the weapon he had
mastered. Starling carried a gun like everybody else,
but he carried it only to back up the firepower of his
steel-shafted arrows, the tips packed with black powder primed to explode on impact. Starling knelt in the
darkness, taking cover next to his bike. He waited.

Bonner took the ice-crusted canvas cover off the
firing mechanism of his .50-caliber machine gun. He
clipped a belt of ammunition into the auto-feed and
leaned against the rollbar. The snow beat him about
the head, catching in his hair.

The lights grew brighter. Big tough men, thought
Bonner, bent low over their bikes, just like those
raiders on the lake bed, riding hard, determined to
prevail. What they didn't know was that they were
doomed to failure. In a few seconds they were going
to ride into a firestorm that would suddenly heat up a
very cold night.

The engines were louder now.

"Starling," yelled Bonner, "you start it off."

"Will do."

They were closing, the lights splitting the snow,
rushing toward doom. Bonner cocked the big gun.

The growl of the engines drowned out the snap of
Starling's bow. The first arrow dashed into the center
of the lights, hit something—man, machine—and blew.
The sheets of falling snow turned a washed-out pink.
A light went out. A man screamed, the tortured
sound rising above howling, racing engines. The headlights shot off at a half-dozen crazy angles. Brakes
wailed.

The long barrel of Bonner's gun started spitting flame. The attackers, whoever they were, were skidding and slipping on the road. The big bullets slammed into chilled flesh and hot blood spurted out onto the snowy road.

Another Starling special exploded in the midst of the tortured mass of men and metal. Bonner twitched the heavy machine gun across the downed riders, sending gouts of paving, blood, and flesh up into the curtains of snow.

The Mean Brothers jumped up, waving their crude weapons. They wanted their fun too.

But to Bonner it wasn't fun. It was part of the code he lived by: kill or be killed.

"Get down," Bonner ordered.

The Mean Brothers hunkered down in their seats, shoulders hunched like chastened dogs.

The big gun continued to chatter, its powerful kick jacking Bonner back and forth as he drew the smoking barrel across the bodies of the dead and dying for a final sweep. You could never be too careful, although it had ceased to be battle and had become instead merely slaughter.

"Think you got 'em," observed Starling.

Bonner stopped firing. Snowflakes drifted down onto the gun and melted.

"Now, let's find out who the fucks are," said Starling. He and Bonner, trailed by the Mean Brothers, advanced. Bonner held his Steyr ahead of him, ready. Starling's fist was filled with a huge Dan

Wesson Magnum. Both were ready to start blasting again.

A groan broke from the shattered body of one of the riders. Bonner knelt by him and looked at the wide exit wound that stained the man's back. It was as wide as a pie tin and the fibers of the man's heavy coat had knit themselves into his slashed flesh. Blood, thick as gravy, poured out onto the frozen road. Bonner figured he had about three minutes to live.

Starling kicked over a body and stared, not altogether sure he could believe his eyes. "You see what I see?"

Bonner nodded. "I see it."

Starling wandered around and kicked over a few more bodies. "See? Every single one of them."

"Yep," said Bonner.

"I'm surprised they fought with lights in a snowstorm."

Experience had taught Bonner that the best men could oftentimes be relied upon to do the wrong thing, to make the move that would lead to their being brought down.

"They're Lightning squadsmen from the Snowstates," said Bonner. "They only fight in the snow. They probably got cocky. They figured we were no-account raiders on the road too late in the season."

"What is the squad doing in the Slavestates?"

Bonner was silent a moment. Listening. On the edge of the snowy breeze came the sound of a lot of engines.

"It doesn't matter," said Bonner. "There are plenty of them out there."

Starling listened. "You know, you might be right."

"Time to go," said Bonner.

"Right again," said Starling.

=================================Chapter Eight

They were still riding when the late dawn broke. The snow had redoubled in intensity and the pearly light of morning did little to improve visibility. Bonner felt fatigue cutting into his bones. Both he and Starling were worn out from the cold and the lack of food. The lightening sky suddenly made Bonner realize just how long he had been riding. He had no idea how much ground he had covered, but he felt as if he was welded to his steering column as he negotiated each twist and turn in the road without a thought. They were riding now on pure guts, instinct, and muscle.

To break the hypnotic spell of the road, Bonner slowed down. He wanted to continue, to put as much ground as he could between himself and the snowmen, but he knew that they had to stop soon. Unless he and Starling had a dose of hot food and at least a walk around to start their circulation again, they ran the risk of succumbing to fatigue and frostbite.

He brought his machine to a halt, the snow crackling under his tires. Starling coasted up next to him.

"Man," said Starling, "we gotta stop." His front was a mass of ice crystals and he crackled a little when he moved.

"Yeah. Drain a little gas and start a fire." Bonner pulled a few cans of stew from under the seat. "Throw these on."

The only sound was the wind and that pleased Bonner. Maybe the squadsmen had given up on them. The Mean Brothers were covered in snow, asleep, leaning against one another. The sudden cessation of the car's motion woke them and they climbed out of their resting places, stretched stiffly, and fluffed the snow out of their hairy chests and off their massive arms. They wandered a few feet down the road they had already traveled.

"Don't stray, Meanies," shouted Starling. He had kicked together some odds and ends of debris and doused them with gasoline. The fire flamed up, took hold of the wet wood, more or less, and Bonner could feel the warmth on his cold, chapped face. It felt good. He started feeling better almost immediately.

Starling opened the old cans with a nicked and scarred knife and set them in the fire. Bonner squatted down next to him, sheltering in the lee of an old Toyota.

"I don't hear anything."

"Me neither," said Starling. "Think we lost 'em?"

"No. But they might have lost interest."

"I hope." Starling narrowed his eyes and looked out over the snow-swept landscape. He thought he could see the ruins of a town off in the distance, but he couldn't really tell. "Where are we?" If anyone knew, it would be Bonner.

"Western Penn," he said, "somewhere around a town they used to call Meadeville."

The old stew cans turned black in the flames and soon the ancient brown sludge started to bubble.

"Come on Means," shouted Starling into the mist, "time to eat."

The men-giants came lumbering out of the snow like trained bears. They eagerly hunched over the fire.

"Hungry?" asked Bonner. The Means nodded in unison, their eyes never leaving the smoldering stew. Bonner took two of the cans from the fire, holding the hot containers gingerly in his heavily gloved hands. "Here."

A Mean Brother seized the hot can in his bare hand, raised it to his lips and tossed off the near-boiling stew as if it was fruit punch. His brother aped his movements perfectly. They were finished eating before the two riders started.

"Do you s'pose these guys are human?" asked Starling.

"Does it matter?"

"Only if they ain't on our side."

By way of punctuation one of the Mean Brothers belched a burp as loud as a pistol shot.

Bonner and Starling ate as fast as they could, taking strength from the brown and chunky liquid. It was so hot it burned their throats.

Suddenly Bonner tensed. He sensed it before he heard it. Through the snow the soft rumble intercut with the higher whine.

"Shit. Fuck," said Starling matter-of-factly.

"There are more of them than before."

"Shit. Fuck," reiterated Starling.

"And they're making good time."

"Why us? What do they want with a couple of good ole riders like you and me?"

Bonner looked down the road. The Lightning squad wore white. Their bikes—right down to the tires—were painted white.

"We can't even see the motherfuckers when they get close," said Starling petulantly, as if the snowmen were taking advantage of his great good nature.

"We'll just have to change that."

"What are we supposed to do, say, 'Hey, winter, go fuck yourself'?"

"Something like that," said Bonner. "In the meantime it wouldn't hurt us any to do a little running."

"I'm with you there boss. Meanies, get into the car."

The Mean Brothers hopped onto their perches, looking hopefully over their shoulders at the approaching sound. They wanted to get caught. They wanted to do a little fighting.

Starling and Bonner set off at the same moment, running side by side. They were at speed in a matter of seconds. Starling marveled at the smooth cruise of his big bike. They knew what they were doing once upon a time. . . .

Bonner figured he had a five-mile head start but the Lightning squad was closing fast. He had to think of some way of fighting them on ground they couldn't use to advantage. If you can choose the field of battle yourself, you've given yourself a leg up toward victory. Allow the enemy to make the decision and you're working at beating yourself. A tiny seed of a plan started germinating in his mind. Slowly, it took root and grew.

Surprise them, he thought; he had to find a way to surprise them. Catch them unawares. It had to be in a place where the white-coated soldiers would stand out, where they couldn't blend into the snowy landscape.

Bonner ran over the hard facts. He was outnumbered. Eventually Starling and he would be caught. Well, they had been outnumbered before—they had been caught before—but this time they wouldn't have a chance if they couldn't get a clear shot at their enemy.

Bonner's mind roamed forward over the highway before him. Quickly but carefully, he unspooled the road ahead in his mind, thinking over every mile of it, wondering if there was somewhere that he could use to his advantage. Then it struck him. He smiled and sat back.

Out of the corner of his eye Starling saw Bonner uncoil behind the wheel. The tall rider laughed to himself. The man had a plan. Maybe they weren't saved but at least now they had a fighting chance. A lot of fighting and a lick of a chance.

Another ten miles of cold highway brought them to a major intersection. One road branched off to the north and Bonner held up a gauntleted hand and gestured to his left. Starling gave the thumbs-up sign, and the car and bike, side by side, swept up the snowy road to the north.

A few minutes later, just as the two sets of tire tracks etched in the snow vanished, the most advanced members of the Lightning squad arrived at the fork. They didn't hesitate, pushing their pounding bikes along the same path taken by Starling and Bonner. The rest of the force followed, swiftly vanishing into the clouds of snow.

Bonner heard the scream of the bikes as they made the sharp turn. The Lightning squad was famous for their speed—they moved much faster than the Stormers—and they were at their best when conditions were bad. They ran their bikes on studded tires that cut into the road, holding them steady. Tires—good ones—were the number-one commodity in the Snowstates, far more important there than in parts of the continent that spent a part of their year outside of the snowy season.

The Snowstates were almost always gripped by winter's cold claw. Bonner could never figure out why anyone—even a crazy man like Carey—would want to spill blood and waste ammo defending them.

And, of course, what was a big cadre of Snowstate Lightning squadsmen doing in the Slavestates' Borderlands? Bonner would probably never know.

He pushed his powerful engine on, the bald tires scrabbling madly to find a grip on the slick roads. Ahead of him on the horizon he could just make out his objective. Spread across the landscape was a dark patch, miles wide, that sat like a heavy beard on pasty-white bloodless flesh. With the passing of each cold mile the target became more and more distinct: it was a forest, a big one, but, more importantly, a dark one. The dim light within would swallow up Bonner and Starling, but show the white-suited snowmen in stark relief.

Bonner was ploughing into the built-up snow on the road, throwing up sheets of snow along the side of his vehicle like the wake of a boat. Snow flew down on him and coursed over the Mean Brothers. Starling cut his speed slightly and tucked himself behind Bonner, slip-streaming as Bonner tore a path in the snow.

A single green sign hung over the road, welcoming him to a state park the name of which he didn't catch. Bonner took a chance and floored the car, pushing all eight cylinders up to full power. They roared into the forest and it got dark, as if someone had snuffed out a single candle. The throaty engines echoed through the silent forest.

The aged pine trees hung over the road, their aged

boughs heavy with snow. The road, under this ancient arboreal shroud, was wet and slick but almost free of snow. Bonner slammed on his brakes and they wailed in annoyance. He thought of Lucky a thousand miles behind him. Lucky was always warning him about the brakes. But they caught this time and Bonner skidded to a stop on the slippery road. He was a good forty yards beyond the point at which he had applied the brakes and a thin, precious layer of rubber striped the roadway.

Starling was next to him. "Nice going," he said. "We'll be able to start blasting as soon as they come through the snow."

"Time to put up a wire?"

Starling cocked his head in the direction of the road. "Yeah, if we're lucky."

He pulled a coil of heavy wire from the deep saddlebags that hung on the rear fender of the Harley. "Here," he shouted to one of the Mean Brothers. "Lay hold of that and tie it round that tree trunk."

The Mean Brother padded across the wet cold road and wrapped the wire round a stout tree. A tiny eddy of snow swirled down onto his broad shoulders, dusting the matted reddish hair a silvery white.

Starling, on the other side of the road, pulled the wire taut, measuring it against his own height, placing it just at throat level. Then he lowered it a bit: the Lightning squadsmen would probably be slightly bent over their handlebars.

The engines were getting louder, pounding through the heavy white of the morning. Bonner set up behind his big gun and silently wished he had taught the Mean Brothers the basics of gunplay. He had no doubt that in the fight they would make their presence felt, but two more guns would have come in very handy.

Bonner looked down the barrel of his gun, his fingers resting lightly on the big triggers. Starling held his bow in front of him, an arrow fitted into the bowstring, but he had not yet pulled the bow double.

The snow appeared to get a little dirty. Imperceptible shapes were moving within the cold shroud.

"Bonner?"

"What?"

"There's no way we can take them all. There must be fifty of the fucks."

"I know that."

"So? What do we do?"

"Give them a few exciting minutes, then get the hell out of here."

Starling laughed. "Now that's strategy."

"When we go, stay away from the road. Go through the trees."

"Good thinking," he said. Starling glanced back at the roadway. "Here they come." And he let fly with the first arrow.

It must have plunged through the headlight and into the gas tank gripped between the lead rider's knees, because the white morning exploded suddenly in a sheet of blue and yellow flame. The Lightning squad formation scattered to the left and right but they continued their headlong charge into the woods.

They burst into the gloom and it seemed as if suddenly the dark woods was filled with the sound of a thousand thundering pistons. The sound bounced off the hanging boughs, compressing the noise. The great white riders were silhouetted against the dark woods. They were excellent targets.

Bonner opened up, the big .50-caliber telegraphing its message—death—the weighty bullets slamming into the Lightning squadsmen with fearful accuracy. The long white riding coats turned red.

A bike skidded across the road. An arrow exploded in the midst of a mass of men and machines. The first few bikes were doomed, and Bonner and Starling dispatched them quickly. But the snowmen were a disciplined group. The riders behind the leaders had slowed down and formed up behind their fallen brethren. They had no clear idea of where Starling and Bonner stood, but they fired back round after round into the almost tangible gloom.

The big .50-caliber reaped another harvest of bone and flesh. A rearward squadsman picked out Bonner's position and gunned his bike, careening down the corridor of death at high speed, one hand guiding the bike, the other clutching an M3 grease gun. He fired as he went. Bonner saw him coming and imagined that the man saw himself as something of a hero.

The wire was two inches into his neck before he realized what had happened. He didn't have a lot of time to think about it. The sharp strand cut into the delicate fretwork of bone and muscle. A look of astonishment froze permanently on the snowman's features as the taut guillotine whipped the head right off the fearless, but foolish, rider's broad shoulders.

The headless body toppled from the bike, the white coat already drenched in blood to the waist. The heavy machine flipped over on its side, the engine racing, the rear wheel still churning in gear. The machine lay there and squealed throughout the firelight like a stuck pig. The man's head came down out of the trees, bounced once or twice on the road, then rolled to rest against the body of the first snowman to fall.

Bullets filled the air like bees, and Bonner did his best with his big artillery to force the snowmen to keep their heads down. The heavy slugs slapped into the broken bikes that lay littering the dark street, picking up twisted chunks of metal and gouging them into the bodies of the squadsmen.

When he had run through a belt of ammo, Bonner picked up the lighter Steyr and continued his fire. But the change of weapon, quick though it was, allowed the white-coated riders a moment to creep forward, to win a few paces of ground. Bent almost double, they ran a few steps forward, then threw themselves flat in the ditch by the side of the road, the muzzles of their guns flashing fire and steel.

Starling threw a glance to his left. Bonner was holding his ugly little gun tight against his forearm, cutting up a squadsman who had tried to make for the shelter of the ditch. His H and R rifle flew out of his hands as Bonner's bullets hammered him.

A spray of bullets jagged into the trees around Bonner, pitching slivers and snow into the air.

Starling's Steyr caught a snowman who was trying to creep through the woods, attempting to outflank the two rider warriors.

"They're coming through the trees," yelled Starling.

Bonner picked up two more crawling belly-flat in the snow. Four rounds whipped into them. At first the men just felt a little numb, as if they had knocked into a sharp corner and bruised themselves. Each was congratulating himself on the lucky escape when one caught sight of the other. Their backs were open from shoulder to waist. Each man thought the same thing: he don't look so good. Then they died.

"Time to go," said Bonner.

"I was hoping you'd say that," yelled Starling.

Another couple of snowmen came through the trees. They fell under the weight of the Mean Brothers. The giants dropped unexpectedly from the low tree branches just above the squadsmen's heads. There was a dull flash of ax and shovel, and the snowmen's warm blood pumped on to the frozen ground, thawing it.

Bonner felt a shift in the balance of the battle. If they didn't pull out soon, they were going to get rushed. The squadsmen were building up on the road, like a logjam.

He jammed a fresh clip into the Steyr. "Let's go."

"Good idea," said Starling, and he kick-started the bike with one powerful jump.

"Meanies," shouted Bonner, "it's go time!"

The Mean Brothers tossed aside the mangled remains of the unfortunate snowmen and ran for Bonner's car. The big engine boomed into life; Bonner crunched it into gear and pushed it off the shoulder and into the underbrush.

The snowmen took a second or two to react to the sudden and unexpected flight of their tormentors, and in those precious moments Bonner and Starling dashed into the tangle of dead vegetation. Their churning tires threw up a wash of snow, bushes, and pine needles.

Chapter Nine

If you weren't looking for Bonner's car, you wouldn't have been able to find it. The trouble was the snowmen were looking for it and they were searching the wild, snowy underbrush very carefully.

Bonner and the Mean Brothers sat motionless in the vehicle, listening to the snowmen as they thrashed and cursed in the bushes. Bonner tried to figure out where they were based from the sounds of their voices; he tried to gauge their distance from him and the direction their search was taking them. They were very close and he figured it was only a matter of time before one of them—all of them—stumbled onto the car and their quarry.

Bonner quickly added up and analyzed the factors that were working for him: the snowmen were on foot, having left their bikes fifty or so yards back at the edge of the road. If Bonner got out of this jam in one piece, he would be able to outrun them easily. He could think of only one other factor that might make life easier for him: he had a fair idea where the snowmen were but they had no idea where he was. It was the old element of surprise, the most valuable weapon a man could have, but its worth lay in knowing when—exactly when—to use it. There was a point in every encounter when the right blow delivered at the right time tossed the balance of the fight right into your hands. Strength, firepower, courage—they were worth very little if you didn't use your brains.

The snowmen were drawing closer. The bushes rattled and shook a few feet away, sending little mattresses of snow fluffing onto the damp ground. Bonner felt his muscles key. It was not yet time to reveal himself: it was time for a quick, silent kill. His hand dropped to his knives. The handles were deadly cold, passionless, like the death he was about to deal to a man whose name he would never know.

The bushes thrashed again. With a crackling of branches and ice a snowman burst into the little thicket occupied by Bonner. He stood there a second looking down, unbelieving, into the car. The big knife sailed through the air, like a flesh-eating fish, and whacked to mid-length into the snow's forehead.

The Mean Brothers had had their own plans for the big soldier, but they had been too slow. A split second after the blade entered the snowman's brow, a

Mean swung his shovel and hit the knife handle, driving the blade deep into the man's brain, like a spike.

The Mean shrugged and smiled his idiotic crooked smile.

The snowmen continued to comb the area. They stumbled and cursed and shouted out to one another. Bonner could tell from the tenor of their voices that they were uneasy, unhappy at being caught in the gloom of the forest. The snowmen were open-country fighters. The enclosed, dripping forest spooked them. All they wanted to do was find Bonner, kill him, and get back on the open road.

"Hey," shouted one suddenly, "where'd Georgie go?"

"He's around here someplace."

"Georgie! Hey, Georgie!"

Bonner assumed that it was Georgie who lay sprawled next to the car with a smashed face and a blade in his head. His blood was oozing out onto the bracken.

"Where'd he go?"

"He was over here. . . ." The crashing in the underbrush was moving closer. Bonner readied himself again. The noise increased in volume. There were more coming his way; this time perhaps three. The main snowman force was spread across the whole area. Bonner wondered where Starling was.

The approaching squadsmen caught sight of Georgie's legs, stretched out in the underbrush.

"Hey," said one. It was his epitaph. As one,

Bonner and the Mean Brothers reared up. Bonner's blades flew. Both silver darts cut into the chest of one of the snowmen, slicing into his heart, severing the hard working organ into two pieces. It pumped once or twice more, then failed.

The Mean Brothers handled the other two. The ax swung and chunked into the meaty rib cage of the snowman. The Mean Brother felt the tightly packed bones split and splinter through the shaft of the ax. The shovel cracked into the back of the head of the remaining snowman. The man's brown hair was suddenly a caved-in mass of gray matter and brain fluid. The terrible thud of ax and shovel on human bone seemed to Bonner to fill the forest. How could the others not have heard it?

As he went down, the snowman who had been on the receiving end of the hideous wound delivered by the Mean Brother's ax pulled the trigger of his rifle. It was a purely reflexive gesture, born of a final, tiny, misguided spark of life. A single bullet tore through the underbrush and buried itself in the heavy carpet of snow and pine needles.

Bonner didn't wait to discover the consequences of that single aimless shot. He sparked the big engine into life, its throaty roar echoing through the forest. He slammed the machine into gear and gunned the engine, praying as he did that the car hadn't rested too long on the soft forest floor. He couldn't get stuck now. Fortunately the faithful iron warhorse did not disappoint him, and with the first blast of gas into its eight huge cylinders, it leaped from its leafy lair.

The sudden movement and the screaming roar struck the dumbfounded snowmen as if the car was not steel and rubber but some sort of forest monster, a sleeping creature awakened by their probings. It seemed to be emerging to defend its turf.

Bonner whipped the elegant shotgun from its holster and blasted two snowmen who stood nearby, rooted to the spot by the sudden noise. Their mouths were wide open. The beautiful old Purdy spoke with authority, peppering their surprised faces with shot. Bonner caught a quick flash of red as their faces opened down to the unnatural white of their jawbones. Teeth flew like confetti.

His engine screamed in protest as Bonner took it up to speed on the soft, uneven ground. He changed gear and yanked at the wheel, turning the car in a tight circle. He silently prayed that there were no rocks buried under the snow that would tear out the undercarriage of the valiant vehicle.

He was making for the road. The snowmen were scattered, and since Bonner's sudden, deadly reappearance, they were running hither and thither like ants around a broken nest. But Bonner knew they would regroup soon enough. He wanted to get back onto the road and bomb off into the forest as fast as he could. The car lunged through the underbrush, rocking like a boat in the clutches of a terrible storm. The Mean Brothers hung on to the rollbar and looked around them with interest. The limited emotion they always displayed seemed to suggest that they were enjoying themselves immensely.

The road loomed up ahead. Parked neatly in a row on the snowy avenue were a dozen or so motorcycles. Bonner pointed the prow of his monster car directly at the orderly rank of bikes. He slammed into the first one and the rest fell like dominoes. The car lunged up onto the tangled heap of bikes, crushing frames and engines, puncturing gas tanks, and snapping delicate spokes under its weight. The car lurched to the top of the metal mountain, rocked there for a moment, then Bonner threw his machine into reverse, backed off, and turned onto the road. A piece of a motorcycle snagged on the underside of his car and it was a hundred yards later that it snapped off.

Bonner shot up to speed while bullets snapped through the snow-heavy branches. A snowman stepped out onto the road and stood directly in the path of the onrushing car. Bonner slipped down in his seat, stamped on the accelerator, and smashed into the fool. The force of the blow lifted the snowman off his feet and threw him over the car. He slapped down onto the road behind the fast-disappearing car.

A motorcycle roared up next to Bonner. The Purdy Special jumped into the Outrider's hands. He swung it over the side and looked down its short barrel directly into Starling's horrified face. Bonner lowered the gun. Starling shouted something, lost in the scream of the engines. Bonner could imagine what he was saying. . . .

Behind them, the snowmen were getting smaller and smaller.

They drove all day and by the coming of night

they were still in the forest. They found a campsite that had a few crumbling brick fireplaces dotted about. They had been placed there many years before and were little monuments to a time when Mr. USA wanted to get away from it all and rough it in the woods. Bonner set the Mean Brothers the task of finding some firewood.

A tattered bathhouse stood in the middle of the clearing. It was a two-room affair, one side marked "men" the other "women." Bonner smiled at the delicacy of the old days.

It was musty inside; the rows of chrome shower heads had long since tarnished themselves into rusty dust. The ceramic sinks and toilets were dry and dusty. A fragment of mirror still hung on the wall. Bonner leaned forward and examined himself. Deep hollows, as purple as bruises, showed under his eyes. His skin was sallow and drawn, a night of hard riding and a day of hard fighting showing plain on his hard face. He ran a callused hand through his hair and onto his forehead, as if to erase the fatigue.

Bonner examined the faded writing on the walls. There were crude sketches of naked men and women, artlessly executed. None of the writing made any sense to him: "Disco sux," "Bobby was here 12-19–97," "Amy and Bill 4ever," "Steelers!," "sex and drugs and rock and roll". . . . It seemed to have been a sort of tradition back then, writing on bathroom walls.

Bonner emerged from the room and into the fresh,

dark night. "I don't think we want to stay in there tonight," he said.

Starling stood by the fire. "We ain't gonna get the chance to make up our minds."

With that, a man with a rusty old rifle stepped out from behind Starling. Before Bonner could react he felt the authoritative press of a gun muzzle in his back. The man with the gun on Starling wore a ratty-looking suit of fur pieces and what appeared to be deerskin leggings. Neither man was wearing white so they weren't snowmen.

"Who are they?" asked Starling.

"Beats me," said Bonner. The gun in his back nudged him to silence. Bonner glanced around him and could sense that there were more figures moving around in the dark just out of the circle thrown by the fire. Had there only been two of them Bonner would have considered trying something, but without any idea of the numbers he was dealing with he decided to wait for a better chance to strike for freedom.

As it happened, he didn't need one. From the dark nearby came a deep and very amused laugh.

"*Bon, mes enfants,*" commanded the voice. "These men are my friends." The guards relaxed and stepped away from their captives. Bonner relaxed and spoke.

"Hey, Jean Baptiste, we're still friends, right?"

"You know these guys," asked Starling incredulously. Figures were crowding into the light, all as peculiarly dressed as the first two. They looked like cavemen with guns.

A heavily bearded man pushed his way through the

crowd. He was covered from head to foot in bearskin. "Ah," he said, "Monsieur Bonner." He seized Bonner's hand and pumped it up and down warmly. "Bonner," he said, his voice heavy with an accent that Starling didn't recognize. "Forgive me. My men did not know you."

"No harm."

Jean Baptiste rapped out some orders to the men that had moved in from the darkness. Starling looked quizzically at Bonner. "What did he say?"

"Jean Baptiste, I'd like you to meet a friend of mine. Starling, this is Jean Baptiste, but mostly down here people call him J.B."

The two men shook hands. "How do," said Starling.

"J.B. is the head of this band of riders; they call themselves Les Habitants—"

"The who?"

"They're from way up north, places that make the Snowstates look good. They don't speak the same language as us. French Canadians, they're from the country that used to take up the top half of the continent."

"I heard about people from up north, but I never seen any."

"What are you doing down here J.B.?"

The northman shrugged his burly shoulders. "It is horrible up there now. There is no food, no gas, no powder. We were raided by Stormers and they took the supplies we collected for the winter." He spat. "Now we look for the Stormers and the food. We are not like the people you have down here in Chicago. We have the families and we care for them.''

''How many men do you have down here?''

''Including me, eighteen. Without me, about ten.'' J.B. roared with laughter at his own joke. ''I am a terrible fighter.''

''Terrible?'' said Starling.

''He means good,'' translated Bonner.

Starling was aware of the inquisitive looks of the Habitants. They were staring at his and Bonner's equipment; he could feel their eyes on his Steyr and his Dan Wesson on his hip. ''Bonner, you don't suppose these guys . . . I mean, I know they're friends of yours and all.''

J.B. pulled himself up to full height. ''Les Habitants do not take the things which are not theirs to take already. Unless it is the things of the Stormers, then we take.''

One of Les Habs spoke quickly and volubly. He was a tiny man with long drooping mustaches and a knife so long it seemed to stretch from his belt to his knees. At the end of his unintelligible speech he held his gun out in front of him.

J.B. laughed. ''Louis says that his gun is as good as yours and that with his gun he has killed more Stormers than you have. He says that you will see his skill when we run into Stormers the next time.''

''Lemme see that thing,'' said Starling, taking the gun from the little man. It seemed to weigh fifty pounds. Starling held it close to the fire and examined it carefully. It was the crudest firearm he had ever seen. A heavy length of pipe—the barrel must have been an inch and half wide—had been fitted into a crudely carved stock. The thing appeared to be muzzle-loaded but at the breech a hole had been cut out of the barrel. There was no trigger.

"How the hell does he fire the thing?"

Louis understood the question instinctively and pulled a heavy hammer from his belt. J.B. explained: "He takes the hammer and hits that little hole at the end of the barrel and sets off the charge."

"And *what* does it fire?"

"Anything he can find," said J.B. with a shrug.

"Make sure he stays away from me if we get into a firefight."

"Many of my men have the same such as these."

"Sheesh," said Starling.

"So, Bonner, you and your friend are out late for men who live in the sun all the time. I thought you would be back in the Chicago all nice and warm and safe."

"We're looking for supplies too, and for Stormers."

J.B.'s grimy face lit up. "So my friend Bonner is also looking for the same thing as Les Habitants. But this is perfect and magnificent for you and for us also." He turned to his men and started telling them of the marvelous capacity that Bonner had for killing Stormers. They looked impressed.

"What do you say Star?" asked Bonner. "You want to ride with the Habs for a piece."

Starling stage-whispered: "They fight with those things."

"They're good, Starling."

"I'll take your word for it. I guess we could go along for a piece of road. . . ." He sounded uncertain.

"Excellent," yelled J.B. "Now we must have some food. Louis with his gun he shot a great bear. It is at the camp we have. It is close by here, down a way the road."

"Bear," said Starling.

"Oh," said Bonner, "that reminds me. I must tell you about the Mean Brothers. . . ."

"The *qui*?"

Hearing their names, the Mean Brothers wandered in from the darkness where they were watching the parley between Bonner and Les Habitants. The northerners would never know how close they had come to tasting the steel of the Mean Brothers' terrible weapons.

J.B.'s eye's widened when the giants walked up. "Ah," he said, "the *Mean* Brothers."

"That's what we call 'em," said Starling.

═══════════════════════Chapter Ten

The grinding of gears split the gray morning, and Sallow, the convoy commander, cursed his lead driver.

"You fuck up that gear box," he growled, "and I'm going to make you eat it."

"Sorry," said the Stormer behind the wheel. He didn't sound like he meant it.

Sallow sat in the passenger seat of the forward truck, the leader of a chain of three vehicles that stretched out behind on the road. It was cold in the tight compartment of the ancient GMC and Sallow had to blow on his hands to keep them warm. The heating system had cut out a long time ago and this particular truck hadn't had a couple of holes cut in the firewall the way some had so the cab would be warmed directly by the engine heat. Maybe at the next stop, Sallow thought, he would get one of the boys to chop some holes in the flimsy metal.

Sallow sat back in the broken seat. The elderly springs hurt his ass. He had been uncomfortable since leaving the Cap. Some fucking detail, he thought, and just his luck to draw it. Why did this shit always happen to him, he wondered. It seemed to him that every time Leatherman had a rotten job to do, he had to do it. He was goddamn patrol leader, not a fucking convoy commander. Convoy commanders were just glorified fucking errand boys.

The patrols were out on the snowy roads; Sallow had no objection to riding, but he hated foraging for supplies. The patrols were moving all the time, providing guard duty and scout information. They were moving, and if you moved fast enough, you were a hell of a lot safer than chugging along wet nursing a bunch of slaves.

Jojo, Leather's main counselor, had brought him to Leather and Leather had said: "Sallow, you're on convoy this trip." That's it, no explanation. Jojo, always the diplomat, had told him that Leather needed his best men on the convoys now. The winter was going to be a tough one, he said, and supplies were crucial, blah, blah, blah. . . .

Maybe, thought Sallow, but his survival was crucial too. To him at any rate. The truth of it was, Leather didn't trust the Stormers anymore.

A mile passed. Relax, Sallow told himself, the smugglers, the raiders, all of the riders, they were all tucked up safe in Chi now. Sallow thought about

Chicago for a moment. The place sounded good to him. One of these fine days he was going to cut out for the open city and maybe set himself up as a raider. Sallow had a feeling that it was only a matter of time before Leather's empire came apart at the seams. The only thing holding it together right now was the fact that the other States couldn't get it together enough to challenge Leather . . . and, of course, the fucking freaky Radleps. . . .

Those guys were crazy and they gave Leather the muscle to give orders and make them stick.

That was what told Sallow that Leather didn't trust his Stormers anymore. The convoys carried Radleps now. There was one sitting up on the cab above him, his big Auto Ordnance resting across his knees. Imagine, Sallow thought, putting Radleps on the convoys to watch the Stormers. Man, he told himself, there were Stormers riding with Leather a long, long time before he recruited his first freak. The man didn't trust his old friends anymore. It was the Stormers that had made Leather. They put him in power. And how many of the original ones were still alive? Three maybe; the rest had been brought down or shot by Leather, for "conspiracy," he said.

Sallow thought about the freak perched on the roof above him, imagining his scarred face showing out from underneath his goggles, his clothes soaking up the snow. Sallow knew that if he tried to take the convoy a little to the west, the Radlep would get real suspicious. If he tried to head flat-out for Chicago, the Radlep would blow him away and Leather would award him some broads and booze and probably some huge fucking piece of artillery so the 'lep could take down a couple more Stormers one day. That was the trouble with the 'leps. They were just waiting to die and they didn't very much care who they took with them.

No, he thought, Chicago would have to wait awhile, until Sallow was leading a patrol of Stormers. Stormers he could trust.

Still, Sallow thought, he wasn't as bad off as some. Sitting behind him in the flatbed of the truck were eleven women he had found out here in the boonies. They were huddled together with the cold but when they got to the Cap, things would get plenty hot for them.

Sallow glanced through the little window over his shoulder. Right now they just looked like gray shapeless bundles, trying to shield themselves against the driving snow, trembling from the cold but also from fear of the future.

There was one, thought Sallow, a little chick with dark brown eyes and long hair. He had already fucked her twice and he would give it to her twice more before he got to the Cap. He smiled to himself. Boy, did she hate him. He could see it in her eyes. He remembered her smooth breasts and belly. She kept herself pretty well for a slave. Didn't smell too bad either. Maybe being a convoy jockey wasn't so bad.

Once she got to the Cap she would go into the personal, private harem of Leatherman himself, or maybe in with the Radleps. By the time she was pitched out and sent to the Stormers she would be used and bruised. The Stormers always got second best.

Sallow sat back and replayed his hot, fast fucking of the night before: the firm body, the tits, that long hair that wrapped around you. So she would go the route with Leatherman, or with the Radleps—fucking freaks—but Sallow had her first. Sallow smiled at the memory of it. . . .

Behind the slave truck was a Peterbilt loaded with food. That would come in handy in the Cap, and Jojo— Sallow hated oily, fat Jojo—would tell him what a good job he had done. Big fucking deal. Astern of the empty truck was a truck carrying forty-six drums of gasoline. They would probably use three on the trip and Jojo would probably give Sallow three drums so the Slavestates would be richer by forty drums of gas. Great. That stuff was worth a fortune in Chicago.

But the second and third truck were manned by Radleps and slave overseers. The overseers were pieces of shit. The Radleps were freaks with the best guns Leather could find. He gave everything to the Radleps—radiation lepers—fucking burn victims that were dying anyway, so they agreed that Leather's word was law. In return he gave them everything they could possibly want: all the guns, gas, girls, ammo, and food they could consume. But the freaks had the tough end of the deal. In return for Leather's generosity they had to be ready to die for him. . . . The hell of the thing, Sallow thought, was that those freaky fucking burn victims were absolutely ready to take any risk that Leather told them to.

It was part of the code they lived by: Leather paid, they died. Simple. No one liked Radleps—not even other Radleps. They were as mean as rats. They might get killed in a firefight, but by God you were going to die too. Sallow had seen them take a half-dozen hits and keep on coming; Radleps with limbs blown away, rivers of blood pouring from their torn bodies, still firing, killing until their bodies failed them. Their hearts or lungs had to give out—because their will never would.

Sallow looked out into the snow. They were making terrible time. They couldn't move any faster on the roads than the all-encompassing snow permitted, but, worse than that, they were slowed down by the male slaves. Between the trucks were twenty or so men, each shackled to a chain that trailed from Sallow's lead truck. They sloshed along at little better than a walking pace—they moved, that is, if they hadn't succumbed to the weather and the shitty food. Then, if they gave in to the torments, they dropped and the chain just pulled them along.

At the back of the truck stood an overseer who used his long lead-tipped whip like a scalpel. With a flick or two of that terrible instrument he could open the back of a slave who fell.

If a slave didn't shape up after a mile or two, the overseer would really go to work. The overseers had a way of knowing who was worth saving and who was worth killing. They were expert judges of human flesh—they would rather cut their losses and kill a slave outright than give one a break and see if he might, just might, make the trip to the Cap.

Sallow was a Stormer and he had seen everything, but the first time he had seen a slave whipped to death . . . well, it had made him a little sick. An overseer could handle that whip so well he could just lick little strips off the skin, mile after mile, until the knotty, bloody backbone was laid bare.

Once the bone showed the fun was almost over. Usually then the overseer would really put some muscle into the crack of the leather thong, break a few vertebrae, then, with one powerful slash, break the backbone completely. Then the slave would be cut down—dead, or merely paralyzed—and left on the roadside. If he was still alive, he would either bleed to death, freeze in the winter, or be eaten by animals.

Yes, thought Sallow, next year he would seize a convoy and head out for Chicago. Course, he thought, he had a lot of enemies in Chicago. Well, he told himself, plenty of time to worry about that next year. . . . Bonner might be a problem. But Bonner couldn't be as tough as his reputation. No one was that tough—his raid on the Cap . . . well, that had just been a case of the breaks going his way. No one was so tough that they couldn't be brought down by a bullet in the back on a dark street. Yeah, thought Sallow, I can handle Bonner. And Chicago was definitely in his future.

But he was wrong. Up ahead on the broken, rutted road Bonner and Les Habitants waited. They couldn't see the convoy yet, but they could hear it, they could hear the weary pull of the engines on the old trucks, inching along the cold road.

Seven of the Habs were hidden on an overpass that stretched over the main road. They looked like wild animals hunched over on the bridge clad in their skins and furs. Each pointed his big cannon into the snowy mist, determined to make every shot hit enemy flesh. Just as the convoy passed under the bridge they would open up, raking the three trucks with as much fire as they could muster. After the initial volley, they figured that the convoy would speed up and run right into the combined firepower of twenty guns.

Sallow stared dumbly at the road, slack-jawed. His mind was miles away yet he didn't know that in a matter of seconds it would be even further away, having departed on a journey from which it would not return.

Louis licked his lips and raised his arm, slamming the hammer down onto the flash pan of his uncertain weapon. There was a sheet of flame, and a low deep boom, and the little man was thrown back. The window in front of Sallow turned a sudden stark white. Tiny veins of cracks ran from one side of the windshield to the other. The disjointed glass seemed to hesitate a moment then dissolve in a great wave of crystal chips. Sallow felt the cold air and saw the snow swirl in and suddenly realized he was covered with blood.

"I'm hit!" he screamed at the driver. Thoughts of Chicago were long gone.

But he wasn't. The driver had been hit, thrown back in his seat, his face a twisted mass of flesh, bone, and mucus. The body of the slain Stormer jammed down on the accelerator and the truck growled on. The Radlep on the roof of the cab was blasting at the bridge. A rip of bullets tore into the truck and Sallow saw the Radlep fall down across the hood of the machine, his weapon slipping onto the road.

"Holy shit!" screamed Sallow to no one in particular.

He lay across the driver, yanked open the door, and pushed the bloody carcass out onto the snowy road. Sallow slid over, pushing himself behind the wheel, feeling the still warm blood of the driver soaking his pants, and grabbing hold of the wheel sticky with the dead man's gore. He stepped on the gas and the truck leaped forward.

The Radleps and the overseers and the two or three Stormers were returning fire but Sallow had no idea where they were shooting. He had but one thought: get the hell out of there. Behind him he heard the screams of the slaves as bullets whipped round them. Vaguely he thought that he was going too fast for the slaves that were shackled to his drag chain. Too fucking bad, he thought, and hit the gas even harder.

Louis, up on the bridge, slammed another of his homemade shells into the big barrel of his crude weapon and took careful aim on a Stormer who crouched on the hood of the second truck. He swung his hammer on the dented spot on the breech. There was a crack, a flash, and sheets of black smoke. When the little gunman picked himself up, he noted, with satisfaction, that only a few grisly remains of the Stormer stuck to the hood and cab, a gory little memorial to a tough guy who never fired a shot.

The weight of fire was far too much for the light force assigned to defend the convoy. Starling's Steyr flashed a few times, missing by inches a Radlep who lay beneath the third truck peppering the area with shot. He had already taken down a couple of Habitants. Those damn Radleps are as dangerous as people say, Starling thought. He tossed aside his little semi-automatic and fitted an arrow into his bow. He stepped into the open and let fly. The steel shaft made contact with the bumper just above the mutant's head. It detonated with a blast powerful enough to throw the truck a few inches into the air.

The Radlep was thrown to the side by the blast and the two and half came down on the man's left arm. Even from where he stood, Starling was sure he could hear the snap of bone. He turned his attention elsewhere.

Bonner wondered how many of the walking slaves, now sprawled next to the slack chain, were still alive. A Stormer showed himself and took three rounds of Bonner's bullets in the lungs. Blood welled out of the man's mouth as thick as vomit.

The concrete at Starling's feet was suddenly stirred up as if splattered by angry steel wasps. He swung around, the Steyr at the ready. It was the Radlep.

Trapped under the truck, his arm crushed, no doubt the man was in unbearable agony, but he still found the pain-wracked strength to get off a few wild shots with his remaining arm. Starling shook his head: these Radleps were crazy. The rider greased him, seven bullets thrashing into the man's mottled flesh.

Two overseers reared up from the middle of the huddle of female slaves, their M16s blazing. Bonner dropped one but the other ducked down behind his human shield. Bonner couldn't risk a tear of gunfire without slaughtering a half dozen of the terrified slaves. But the overseer was in there, and while he lived he was trouble.

Bonner was amazed by what happened next. A slave woman stood suddenly and slammed her manacled hands down onto the overseer's head. It was a noble effort but the overseer was a big old cuss and the blow—a light one, the woman was weak from hunger and exposure—glanced off him. But the sudden attack from an unexpected quarter annoyed the man. He turned and fired.

The bullets slammed into the woman at point-blank range, lifting her off her feet, and whipped her back to the cab of the truck. Bonner could see the thin chest of the dead woman open up, twisted and bloody.

A bolt of anger shot through him. Another pointless death, another unhappy painful end to an unhappy life. He jumped out from his cover, the Steyr chattering. Bonner didn't care if he was a target or not. He was going to kill the sonofabitch.

But Bonner had competition. The Mean Brother with the shovel scaled the side of the truck, clambering over the top like a crab. He held the shovel by the shaft, clamped between his big yellow teeth. Deep within his slow brain some innate sense of honor and decency had been awakened. Perhaps it was closer to the surface in a simple man like a Mean Brother than in the "clever" men of the new world. The big man's eyes sparkled with hate. The killing of the defenseless woman had outraged him and he was determined to make sure that the overseer would pay dearly for his act—and the only coin the Mean Brother would accept as payment was pain.

The Mean Brother waded through the crouching women and knocked the overseer's gun from his hands with the heavy shovel. Terror was writ large on the overseer's dirty face. The Mean tossed aside his shovel and reached for the hapless tough guy, his huge hands gathering up the overseer's shirt. He yanked him to his feet. The overseer tried to fight for his life and slammed both fists into the Mean Brother's gut. His hard knuckles struck firm flesh and made no impact on the Mean Brother whatsoever.

An anguished scream tore from his victim's throat as the Mean Brother lifted him effortlessly from the ground. The giant's arms worked as if they were hydraulically powered. He held the overseer over his head, the man howling, mewling like a child, his legs scissoring in the cold air. When the Mean Brother's arms were extended fully, he seemed to jump slightly, then he slammed the overseer down onto the upright side of the truck. He fell across it, his back arched on either side. There was a distinct sound of the splitting and popping of the delicate, dainty bones of the spine.

The overseer toppled over the side to the ground and lay there, his broken body trying frantically to send messages to the brain over the broken highway of his backbone. He couldn't move. He watched as the Mean jumped down from the truck, reached down and pulled the overseer up by the neck. With the man's head tucked into the crook of his arm the Mean Brother smashed it into the side of the truck. Twice, three times, then a fourth. He pounded again and again, as if he was using the man to batter down a stout metal door. The truck rang dully with the thud of bone on steel. He only stopped when it appeared that he was holding a pot of meat in his arm. Then he tossed the shattered body aside, his hairy arms dripping with gore. As he stooped to retrieve his shovel he caught sight of Bonner and the terrified women. The Mean Brother shrugged.

The battle had come to an abrupt halt. The Stormers, Radleps, and overseers lay scattered about. J.B. came wandering out from the culvert where he had been secreted and his men came down from the bridge.

"It is a good thing, this convoy, I think," he said laconically.

"How many men did you lose?" asked Bonner.

"I think maybe four. They fight like hell, these Radleps."

"Yes," said Bonner, "they do."

"And those large men with you, *mon dieu*." He waved his hand back and forth. "What terrible men for the fighting . . ."

Les Habitants were climbing over the trucks, jabbering away, excitedly examining the spoils. "There is much here," observed J.B.

Starling looped over. "What do you want to do with them?" He jerked a thumb over his shoulder at the women.

"Any of their menfolk alive?"

"One, but he won't last the night. All of 'em got dragged when we started firing."

Bonner exhaled heavily and walked over to the women. They stared at him wide-eyed, wondering if he was a rescuer or just another tormentor. Bonner himself didn't know.

"Where are you from?" he asked gently.

"Down the road," said one hesitantly, "down the road, that way." She gestured vaguely.

"Far?"

She shrugged. "Dunno."

Bonner kicked the dirt by the road. He couldn't take them with him—they would get killed, probably. He couldn't leave them here—they would die of exposure, probably. It was a toss-up. If he left them supplies, maybe they would try to get to the next rubble village. What would happen to them after that . . . that was anybody's guess.

"Are you going to hurt us?" asked a girl timidly.

"No," said Bonner. "You are going to have to

stay here.'' It was a difficult decision, but he had to do it.

"But," she stammered, "but we'll die." The women set up a chorus of complaints.

"We're going to leave food for you. You'll make it okay." Bonner recognized the futility of his words and hoped the women did not. Maybe it would have been better if they had all caught stray slugs in the firefight. Now, he knew, they would stay there, under the broken overpass until their food ran out. Then, nature would claim them, slowly, painfully.

Les Habitants usually traveled piled onto a broken-down old rust bucket of a truck driven by J.B. It was an ancient mongrel hulk that always seemed to be on the verge of complete, irrevocable breakdown. After a hurried consultation among themselves, they decided to trade in their old steed for one of the convoy's more trustworthy vehicles. They loaded it methodically.

"Time to go," said Starling.

"Mais non," protested J.B. "First we must bury our dead. It is a thing we always do, us."

"Yeah, sure," said Starling, knowing it was just a matter of time before the wolves scented the bodies and dug them up.

Digging was hard in the frozen ground, and by the time four graves were dug and filled in, night was coming on. Bonner decided they should move anyway. He didn't want to spend the night with the women around. They made him uncomfortable.

As the little convoy made its way down the road Bonner could feel the women's eyes on him through the gloom, watching him, coldly accusing him of sentencing them to a long and lonely death.

Chapter Eleven

Leatherman looked evil. Part of this was pure show; he cultivated his mean-looking image, but it would be a mistake to assume that underneath that nasty-looking face there was something other than pure meaness.

He always wore leather pants, soft and supple leather that was specially cured for him. These were thrust into heavy black boots that reached the knee. His broad hairy chest was covered by a leather shirt that was laced with a hide thong down the front. To ward off the cold he wore a full-length cowhide overcoat with a high collar that framed his head.

He was a tall man and ugly to boot. He had fat, fleshy lips, and there was a hard look in his left eye that admitted no pity. His right eye was covered by an eye patch. An angry red scar, as deep as a fissure in a rock face, ran from his forehead, straight down behind the eye patch, then continued down his cheek, branching out into three jagged cuts on his strong chin. Dara had done that, and you only needed to see the scar to sense the hate that had driven the blow that had so horribly disfigured him. But he had settled his scores with Dara. She had hurt him, but he made her pay him back tenfold, in blood, humiliation, and ultimately in death.

Leather had no hands. In their place he had fitted to his stumps wooden blocks that capped his tortured arms. In the wooden blocks he had had fitted Bonner's knives. Two of the blades protruded from the right stump, and the third was set in his left. If Bonner had taken Leather's hands, so Leatherman had replaced them with Bonner's blades, something that gave him great satisfaction. It was almost as if he had fitted himself with pieces of Bonner's soul. Leather prided himself on his sense of humor.

But recently, things had not been going Leather's way. Since Bonner's devastating raid on the Cap, he'd had troubles.

The Stormers were getting harder to control; they were essentially mercenaries who were prepared to go along with him when things were rosy, but they got nasty when things weren't going so well. Stormers had taken most of the hits from Bonner, though God knows, the Radleps had found their force reduced by a substantial number. But the 'leps were loyal. They loved Leather. Most people that bothered to think about it figured they loved him for his unstinting generosity with them when it came to the stuff that the rest of the world hungered for. But Leather was no fool. He knew if the Radleps wanted that stuff, they would have just taken it and there was very little anyone could have done to stop them. No, Leather gave them something, something that all the gas, girls, and guns in the world couldn't have provided. Leatherman gave them pride, and in return for that they were prepared to die for him.

Leather was on the road now, lolling in the backseat of his bright red jeep at the head of a Radlep battalion. Jojo, his chief counselor and adviser, had convinced him that going out on the road personally would be a good move: inspire the troops and frighten the slaves, that sort of thing. And of course, there was the matter of finding the gas farm they had heard about. They needed that gas bad.

Stretched behind the jeep was a Radlep force that Leather had personally chosen to accompany him. Seventy-five of the big ugly men fanned out behind him on their huge bikes. They wore goggles to protect their eyes from the snow; they rode hunched over the bars of their motorcycles, their weapons strapped across their backs.

Leather slouched back in his seat and looked at his driver Chilly. He was about the ugliest Radlep he had ever seen. The folds of skin on the young man's thin neck were calloused and brown, like the skin of a reptile. His hair had fallen out and his bald head was crisscrossed with tears and lesions. His eyes stared out from deep sick-looking sockets; he looked along tunnels of decaying flesh. His nose was collapsing, its thin bones caving in as they were eaten away. The man's mouth was the usual Radlep raw wound of cracked and torn lips and broken teeth.

Leather could tell by the awkward cast of Chilly's body under his greatcoat that another limb, probably a stunted arm, was growing out of the chest cavity. It was a common condition among the Radleps. Chilly was Leather's personal bodyguard, a ferocious, tenacious fighter, so devoted to him Leather doubted if there was a thing he wouldn't do for his master if Leather asked it. Strapped to Chilly's waist was a Browning 9mm Hi-Power, and Leather knew that he could tell Chilly to take it out, put the barrel in his mouth, and pull the trigger. Chilly would do it, simply because Leather ordered it.

Chilly leaned toward the cracked windshield and squinted. "Boss," he rasped, and lifted a gloved hand off the wheel to gesture forward on the road.

Leather looked. Far ahead he could just make out a couple of riders. "Who?"

"Charlie and Sam," said Chilly.

"Good." Leather relaxed. His scouts were returning. "Maybe they got some news for us."

The scouts and the main force met a few miles further up the road. A few fat flakes of snow were falling and they promised a lot more snow. The exhaust from all the bikes, the supply trucks, and the jeeps mingled with the cold breath of the men. The entire column was engulfed by a damp, gray cloud.

Leatherman hoisted himself out of the seat and dropped down onto the concrete. He walked stiffly; they had been driving since dawn. "So what you got, Charlie? Any sign of the gas?"

The scarred scout pushed up his goggles. His extremely sensitive skin was raw where the goggles had pressed against his flesh. "No gas. Snowmen up ahead."

"Snowmen?" said Leather. "What the fuck are they doing here?"

Charlie shrugged. "They're here." But every man in the column knew why they were here. They had heard that Leather was weak and they had been sent to see if maybe the Slavestates weren't ripe for conquest.

"How many?"

"Thirty, maybe a few more." Charlie hocked up and spat.

"How far?"

"Five-six miles," said Sam.

"They on the road?"

"Yeah. Headed this way too."

"Good, let's take the fucks," said Leather. If Carey sent out some squadsmen and none came back, that should let him know just how weak Leatherman was.

The Radleps gunned their engines and pounded down the road, springing forward like a pack of hounds hot for the kill. The forthcoming firefight would warm up the drab, dull, cold morning.

A couple of riders attached themselves to the side

of Leather's jeep, riding escort. They knew that without hands their leader was helpless.

The Lightning squadsmen saw them coming. The
Radleps roared over a rise in the road and the snowmen
saw the first wave followed by several more.

"Holeeee sheeeeeet," said the lead snowman, brak-
ing suddenly.

His men stopped around him. "Boys, it looks like
this just ain't our ride, you know what I mean?" It
was the same group of riders who had encountered
Bonner and Starling. "So what to do?" he asked.

"Man," said one of them, "I wanna live a little
longer."

"What's your second choice?" They were deep in
slave territory with no hope of reinforcements. They
could stand and fight and most likely get sliced, or
they could run and probably end up sliced anyway.

"It ain't that guy again, is it?"

"Nawwwww."

"Then fuck it, let's take 'em."

The two forces barreled toward them, charging
like the cavalry of old. As the two bands met there
seemed to be a sound of clashing steel echoing out
over the valley. Brakes were applied, engines wailed,
the air was filled with a heavy boom and the sharp
crack of sidearms of every type and caliber. Men
fell, shooting gouts of blood into the crisp air. Bikes,
riderless, shot here and there a few feet then toppled
over, some still in gear, driving around in crazy
circular patterns.

This was war on wheels. Snowmen and Radleps

sat astride their steel steeds, one hand gripping the handlebars, the other arm outstretched, gun in hand, blasting at their enemies. The riders completed their first pass, turned in tight circles, then urged their bikes on for another encounter.

A snowman and a Radlep collided, the two bikes jamming together in a tortured confused mixture of metal and meat. They fell, the snowman cracking his head painfully on the cold concrete. He lay dazed while the mounted riders wheeled and fired around him. He was unable to rise.

The Radlep flew into the air and fell with a thick, sickening thud. Immediately a bike rolled over his chest and he felt his ribs crack, splinter, and give way under the weight of the heavy cycle and rider. His lungs shattered by the sharp shards of his own shattered bones, he still managed to unsling his M16. He tasted the sweet taste of his own blood in his mouth, curling around his tongue. He lay flat on his broken chest, ignoring the pain, and took careful aim on the swirling riders. He fired methodically, the big steel-jacketed slugs thumping into snowmen. He took down seven squadsmen that way until a stray bullet—Radlep, snowman, who knows—tore off the back of his hairless head.

Chilly had pulled the jeep up onto a rise overlooking the highway and he stood up, leaning on the windshield a chattering M3, accounting for about a dozen snowmen. Leatherman sat and watched. As far as he could tell, there just weren't enough snowmen to go around. It was an uneven battle from the start, and the odds against the snowmen were lengthening with the passage of each bloody second. Leather watched the battle with the fine eye of a connoisseur. Carey, the Prince of the Snowstates, as he called himself, had trained his men well. But he had not done such a good job that his men could come wandering into the Slavestates, take on twice their number in Radleps, and live.

What the fuck were they doing here anyway? He jammed his elbow in Chilly's ribs. "I want one. Alive."

Chilly nodded and jumped down from the jeep. He tossed his weapon into the backseat and drew out an old number-one-iron golf club. "Somebody special you have in mind, boss?"

"That guy there," announced Leather, pointing out a snowman, who, still mounted on his motorcycle, was racing across the road.

"Got it," rasped Chilly. He strode into the furious storm of men and bikes, walking casually, as if he was taking a morning stroll. He took a few short practice strokes with the club. He paused as the squadsman that Leather had pointed out tore toward him. Just as he passed, Billy whipped the light club into the man's gut.

The snowman's cheeks filled with air as the fist-sized head of the club burrowed into the flesh of his abdomen. The blow seemed to stop him in midair, arresting him in a dead halt. The bike raced on for a yard or two, then fell over. The snowman followed his bike to the ground, falling in a bundle wrapped around the club at Chilly's feet. Chilly scooped the big man up, slung him over his shoulder, and carried him nonchalantly back to his master.

"Nice work," said Leather. Chilly beamed.

Like a gasoline fire, the battle burned high and hot for a moment then died down quietly. The snowmen lay strewn about the road and the shoulder; the dead or soon to be were quickly being covered with a fine blanket of snow. A Radlep walked from body to body, checking to see if any still lived. Those who still groaned or gulped for air or dazedly tried to crawl away received a bullet in the head. The Radleps were nothing if not efficient. It was a parting gift, Radlep style.

The sole remaining snowman, Chilly's captive, leaned back against the tire of Leather's jeep, holding his gut, still gasping for breath.

"Stand him up," ordered Leather.

Chilly grasped the man by the shoulder and forced him to his feet, pulling him back by the hair, stretching the painfully bruised stomach muscles. The snowman looked at Leather with hate-filled eyes. It was cold, but big beads of sweat had popped out on his forehead.

"Well," said Leather, sitting comfortably in his seat, "what's your name?"

The snowman looked over Leather's torn face. "Fuck you, freak."

Leather's right hand whipped out savagely, carving two fine gashes across the snowman's cheek.

Blood spread down his cheek and he yelped and tried to bring a hand up to his face.

"Now, what's your name?"

The squadsman stared at the claw that Leather held forward.

"Jackie."

"Well, Jackie, what the fuck are you doing in my country?"

"Carey," stammered Jackie, "Carey sent us. . . ."

"I know Carey. Me and Carey go way back. Now why would Carey send a nice boy like you all the way to the Slavestates? Didn't he tell you that you'd wind up dead? Didn't he tell you about my Radleps and my Stormers? And look how many guys he sent . . . look at that." He gestured toward the slain snowmen. "Why, there ain't thirty guys there."

"There were more of us," said Jackie.

Leather smiled broadly. "Now you're talking, sonny boy, where are they now?"

"Dead."

"Dead? Who killed them? 'Leps? Stormers?"

"Dunno. Some guys . . ."

"You're pissing me off, Jackie," said Leather, as if he was disciplining a child. "You're making me mad."

"Sorry," said Jackie.

"No, son, don't be sorry. Just tell me. Who took your other guys down?"

"Four guys. Four guys in a forest upstate from here."

"Four?" Leather leaned forward. Could it be, he wondered. "Four riders? How many did they get?"

"Dunno. Twenty maybe."

"Four guys, twenty snowmen?"

"That's right," stammered Jackie. Then, as if to apologize for such a lopsided score, he added, "Man, these guys were *tight*. They acted like there were more of them than us. We never seen anything like it."

"One of these guys," said Leather slowly, "did he have three blades on his hip? And a shotgun? And a haul-ass car with a big chattergun on the back?"

"Yeah," said Jackie, "who is that fuck? Your secret weapon."

"Don't talk to me that way, boy," said Leather, and his right hand whipped out again, only this time the double blades caught Jackie deep in the throat. A fine spray of blood came first, then, as pressure opened the wounds, a waterfall of gore coursed out. Jackie's young face drained of color immediately and his eyes rolled back in his head. He fell forward on the jeep.

"Chilly," said Leather calmly, evenly, "you wanna get this fuck off me. He's bleeding all over my shoes and everywhere."

But inside, Leather was trembling, and there was only one thought on his mind: Bonner was back.

=Chapter Twelve

Bonner and Les Habs slid out onto the cold road just after dawn. The morning was bright and clear, a welcome relief from the bad weather they had been driving in almost since they set out on the road in Chicago. The engines sang in the fresh morning air and Bonner allowed himself to slip back in his seat and, for a moment, to enjoy the clean cold morning.

They were riding through country that was made up of tall hills and deep valleys, dusted with the new white of a fresh snowfall. The road was curved but open, almost completely free of hulks and wrecks although those ubiquitous rusting landmarks could be seen from time to time pushed over by the side of the highway. Periodically they passed through or around the ugly wound of an old mill town. The little convoy passed slowly through the rubble, their big engines echoing off the broken walls. There was nothing that Bonner had ever seen that was quite as dead as a dead town. They saw no slaves, they were still too far north.

But Bonner knew that they were sure to run into people soon. The further south they drove, the more likely they were to run into slaves and slaves meant tax men and tax men meant Stormers.

Each part of Leather's empire had been divided into sectors, each commanded by a tax general who was likely to live in the Cap. The tax general was in charge of seeing that his sector provided the quota of supplies that Leather and Jojo had decided it could produce. The figures were often impossibly high, and the tax generals were always worried about meeting their quota. Leather knew the value of his administrators, so if you missed your quota once or twice he would probably let it ride. If you missed it often enough, he gave a curt order to a handy Radlep and the 'lep blew your head off.

But a tax general could get rich if he worked at it. They said that the richest men in the Slavestates were the tax generals, one or two of them even rivaling Leather himself. Each general was allowed to take a cut of the goods his sector produced.

Executing the commands of tax generals were the tax soldiers. Each sector was divided into regions and each region was looked after by two tax men. The tax soldiers worked with the slaves, squeezing the slaves as hard as they could. It was up to them to make sure that the slaves worked eighteen hours a day in the fields and the mines, tending livestock and foraging for the supplies that had been left over when the old world vanished in a cloud of fire and death. Like the tax generals, the tax soldiers were allowed to take a piece of the spoils, so they worked hard and they worked their hapless slaves harder. It was a job that demanded constant and absolute ruthlessness: you couldn't have a soft heart and make any money, that was a rule.

The tax men had to work hard to meet their quotas. Out of the stuff provided by their region, the tax soldiers had to ensure that there was enough food to support the slaves and the Stormer units that traveled the area, the Stormers in turn ensuring that the tax men could work at their rape and pillage of the land without interruption. Each sector paid for itself and tax men were not above cutting rations to the slaves to increase their quota and their own profits. Tax soldiers weren't popular men.

Bonner's force was heading south toward the ruins of an old mill town that sat deep in the mountains. At the old ruined railroad station a cracked sign read: ALTOONA. Bonner had agreed to meet Seth there, just to check in and compare notes.

From old Cooker's cackling information, they figured their goal was somewhere in that region. Of course, they might be off by five hundred miles; maybe the old gas hound was simply telling a big lie, something to amuse the boys around the campfire.

Gas hounds weren't famous for being real stable mentally. But that was a risk you took when you went smuggling. They might go thrashing around in the snow for three long, cold weeks, ducking patrols, fighting, and still come up empty-handed. It was an uncertain way to make a living, a dangerous one too, but vastly preferable, or so thought Bonner and Starling and men like them, to taking orders from another man, to do another man's bidding.

Bonner was in the lead with Starling riding beside him. The heavy truck carrying Les Habitants rumbled along behind them. Bonner had been curiously moved by the simple laying to rest of the slain Habs. The Canadians had buried their comrades without any real ceremony, simply laying them in their cold holes in the frozen ground and covering them with dirt. The men then stood there a moment or two in silence, the dirty windblown snow whipping around them. Starling and Bonner had stood away a bit, at a distance, feeling a little awkward, as if they were unwelcome intruders at a private, family gathering. As Les Habitants dispersed, all of them had a tear or two in their eyes, but Bonner could also see that they now had new resolve to fight on, to destroy their enemies and avenge their noble, fallen comrades.

Someone had pushed the old Hab truck over the graves, a rusty, but fitting memorial to the men whose bodies would decay and vanish, but whose memories would live on in the minds and actions of their comrades. As soon as the ceremony was over the remaining Habs decided quietly among themselves who would care for the families of the fallen. It touched Bonner. They lived together and fought together for the good of them all, for the good of a single tight-knit unit. They were good men and they lived by the gun, but they believed in virtue.

Watching the funeral, Bonner was reminded that he hadn't been able to bury Dara. . . .

The sunny freshness of the day contrasted starkly with the dark mood that had crept over Bonner. He toed the gas pedal a touch harder and silently prayed that Leatherman was out there somewhere.

They rode another twenty-five miles, and for every inch of it Bonner tried to drive his melancholy and his shame from his mind. He failed. So engrossed was he in his thoughts and his private musings that it was Starling who first saw that, up ahead on the highway, a rusting hulk of an old Datsun had been pushed lengthwise across the road. He cut speed immediately.

The sudden change of the engine note a few yards from Bonner's ear jerked him back to reality. He saw the car, realized the danger, and hit the brakes, swerving to a stop at the side of the road. The Habs threw on their brakes and pulled up slightly behind him. Starling was on the far side of the road.

"Bonner," shouted Starling.

"Yeah."

"What do you think?"

"I know a roadblock when I see one."

"Whose you s'pose it is?"

"Stormer, probably."

"So what do you want to do?"

"Take a closer look." Bonner unslung the Steyr and held his shotgun in the other hand. He stood up slowly and advanced cautiously toward the wreck. There was no movement behind or around it. Bonner doubted that there was a hornet's nest of Stormers crouched behind the old burnt-out shell of a car. More likely the hulk was a maze of booby traps and other assorted dangers.

"Hey Bonner," shouted Starling, "look out for mines."

Bonner's eyes swept the ground ahead of him. A few inches of snow covered the ground. He could see no sign of the white carpet having been disturbed. There were two telltale signs of mines: a rough bit of ground where a mine had been carelessly placed with no attempt to hide it and a spot where the ground appeared to be unnaturally smooth—where the miner had been too careful, too meticulous in camouflaging his dirty work.

Bonner stepped carefully, placing his feet in the snow with caution, waiting to hear the telltale "chunk" that meant he had stepped onto a spring-loaded weight mine. If he tripped the spring, he had to resist the natural and involuntary impulse to step off immediately. While he held the spring down he was safe. As soon as he stepped off he would blow himself to pieces.

But no sound came. As he got closer to the wreck he paused, his two guns held out before him. Then he sprinted the last few yards and jumped up onto the rusty hood. He stood there a second looking over the hulk. Then, suddenly, a huge pair of arms swept up and grabbed him around the boots and pulled him down behind the car.

As soon as he vanished, the Mean Brothers were off and running, pounding across the snow, waving their weapons, their eyes set and blazing like bird dogs', not taking them from the spot where Bonner had disappeared. They didn't care about mines and their huge feet threw up large gouts of snow as they ran.

"Means!" screamed Starling. "No! No!." He expected to hear the chatter of murderous fire open up and cut down the big brothers. But there was no stopping them. And there was no gunfire either.

A few feet from the Datsun the Mean Brothers jumped, flying off the ground and going headfirst over the dented nose of the wreck.

Starling and the Habs stood dumbstruck for a moment and then started running toward the car. "What the fuck is going on?" yelled Starling.

With that came a sound that echoed from behind the car. It was a sound that Starling knew extremely well; he slowed down and put his hands disgustedly on his hips.

"Haw haw haw haw." A deep throaty laugh seemed to echo out of a deep granite crypt. With that signature laugh it could be no one else. Beck rose up from behind the car, one of his huge arms thrown across Bonner's shoulders. Beck's wide face was bright with amusement. Bonner smiled. Even the Mean Brothers looked pretty happy.

"Beck," screamed Starling, "are you fucking crazy?

We were fixin' to blow your dumb-shit, peckerwood, motherfucking head off. You dumb shit. We would have cut you into a million fucking pieces. You stupid shit! Goddamn!''

Beck's deep voice: "Not in front of the children, Starling. Watch your fucking mouth." And he laughed some more: "Haw, haw, haw."

"The Mean Brothers would have taken you apart," screamed Starling.

"The hell they would," bellowed Beck. "These little tykes couldn't damage a fucking kitten."

Beck was a giant of a man, standing a good foot taller than the Mean Brothers. He was seven feet if he was an inch, and mostly muscle. He did have a big gut that hung down over his wide brass-buckled leather belt. He had four or five belts of heavy-caliber ammunition crossed on his massive barrel chest. Lank black hair fell to his broad shoulders. His thick legs were planted firmly on the ground, like bulky, knotty tree trunks. He had teeth the size of small tombstones and they were permanently stained brown. Everyone knew this because Beck laughed so much and always showed his ugly teeth when he did.

"Mon Dieu," said J.B. "This man would take plenty of the killing, *non?"*

"Nobody gonna kill me, buddy. I ain't going until I decide, and lemme tell you that time ain't come yet," bellowed Beck. "And who the hell are you anyway and why the fuck do you talk so strange. You picked up another bunch of freaks, Bonner?"

"Jean Baptiste," said Bonner, "this is Beck."

"Big fucking deal. How come he talks funny?"

"I am from the north. If you were up there, it would be us, Les Habitants, that would be saying that you were the one who would be talking funny."

"Didn't understand a fucking word," said Beck. "All these guys, they with him?"

"Right," said Bonner. "Allow me to introduce the Habitants."

"The who?"

"Forget it. What you doing out here, Beck?"

"I was outbound for Chi. I was just doing a little late-in-the-season looking around, you know what I mean? Stormers all over the fucking place. 'Leps too. I took out a few small patrols, but the big ones, forget it. I'm none too popular in the Cap, you know. . . ." Beck had been a latecomer to the raid on Washington that Bonner had commanded, but he had managed to take Leather for twenty thousand gold slates. He was almost as high as Bonner on Leather's hate list. "Why are you out?"

"Little hunting," said Bonner.

"Oh yeah? Hunting what?"

"Gas."

Beck smiled broadly. "Well," he said, "I'm all ears. Tell me about it Bonner."

Bonner turned to Starling and J.B. "We got room for one more?"

"Sure," said Starling with a shrug of his shoulders.

"*Pourquoi pas?*" said J.B.

"Hey, no don't do me no favors, you pricks. You need me more than I need you."

"What means this?" said J.B.

"What means this, mister, is that I been down that road and I know where the 'leps and Stormers were and probably where they're going. You gotta gun me in for a lotta that gas."

"You get the same share as everybody else," said Starling.

Beck grinned. "Awwwwww, Star, my man, I didn't say I wanted anything but a fair share. I'm just an old softy. Besides I want another crack at the Stormers. It ain't cold enough to hunker down in Chi town yet."

They drove without incident until nightfall. When they stopped for the night Bonner spoke to Beck privately.

"So you been down this road?" he asked quietly.

"That's right."

"Lots of Stormers?"

"Stormers, 'leps, convoys, patrols, you name it. It's a fucking doom-freak salad out there."

"Any sign of Leather?" Bonner asked casually.

Beck looked knowingly at Bonner, his eyes glittering in the dark. "Still got that splinter in your ass, huh Bonner?"

"Something like that."

"Well, this'll cheer you up. I heard he's out there."

"Good," said Bonner.

Chapter Thirteen

Seth cleared the firelands in good time, although he had paused to forage for coal that had not yet been consumed by the constant fire. He found what he needed and moved on.

Most riders wouldn't go near the firelands; those few that knew their way through, or at least thought they did, only entered the inferno when they absolutely had to. But Seth wasn't like that; as he pulled out of the gray-black clouds he almost hated to leave. Once he left the billows of smoke behind he knew he was a target. In the firelands he was safe, safe from other men at any rate.

The old engine rattled along the rusty tracks, and for the first time in days Seth could step back from the hot boiler and feel, not the hot supercharged air of the firelands, but instead, the invigorating sting of cold winter winds. He pulled the bandanna off his mouth and breathed fresh air.

He set the throttle and bent his whip-hard body to the task of stoking the furnace with coal. He worked like a machine, turning from the coal hod to the roaring furnace that showed through the open door with load upon load of coal. When he had moved a few hundred pounds of coal, Seth tossed aside his shovel and went for a stroll.

He climbed over the glittering black mountain of coal stored in the hopper behind him, dropped down onto the flatbed that rode behind the engine, and climbed up onto the the first of the three shiny silver tank cars that trailed behind the locomotive like obedient mongrels. He climbed and jumped to the furthest point on the last car. He settled down there and rooted around in the breast pocket of his heavy workshirt for a cigar. He found the lumpy, foul-smelling tube made of trash tobacco that the raiders brought in sometimes from down south and he lit it with an old flint lighter that he had found in the station master's office of an old station in Tularosa, New Mexico, down in the Hotstates.

An elaborate design spelled out the name of the old line: ATCHESON, TOPEKA, AND THE SANTA-FE. Seth treasured it because it was a long, delicate thread stretching back to the railroad men of ancient times. He blew out a line of blue smoke and watched while it drifted up and mixed with the heavier puffs his old iron maiden was throwing off.

Seth was about as close as you could get to contentment. He had few enemies, no burning hatreds, and a few good friends: Bonner, Starling, Dorca . . . He was tough and fast and he used his stark little M3 like a master. He owed no man allegiance, except maybe Bonner. The Outrider had saved Seth's ass more than once. . . . But Seth had done the same for Bonner. They figured it all evened out in the end, although sometimes they playfully teased one another: "What about the time I pulled you out of the firelands? Man, you would have been dead meat if it hadn't been for me. . . ."

Seth leaned back. Yeah, contentment was what you called it.

Hunger, the leader of a Stormer patrol, held up his gloved hand and slowed his band of machines and men to a crawl. Sonny, his second-in-command, coasted up next to him. He pushed up his goggles.

"So what's up?"

"Look," said Hunger, pointing over the tree line. About two miles off big puffs of smoke were appearing in the morning sky at regular intervals.

"What's the fuck dat?" said Sonny.

"I'll tell you what the fuck is that," said Hunger. "It's that fucking nigger with the wild steam box."

"Hey, far fucking out, let's take him."

"Okay," said Hunger affably. He slipped his brake and roared off, his band behind him whooping and screaming for blood.

*   *   *

Seth was still perched out on the end of the tank when the first bullets pinged and flattened themselves on the steel piece of rolling stock.

"Damn," he whispered, ducking down on the rear bumper. Then he realized he had left his little M3 hanging next to the throttle three cars ahead of him. That wasn't like him. Contentment breeds complacency, and that, Seth decided, was not such a good thing: it could get a man killed.

He only had his old Charter semi-automatic Explorer .22, a light gun with an eight-shot clip—Seth didn't hold much with sidearms—but he had no idea where the shots were coming from. He left the .22 in its holster and slipped under the tank truck. It was like coming in out of the rain. The bullets continued to ping and richochet around the topside of the tank, telling Seth that his attackers had no clear idea of where he was. But he was in a jam.

He hung beneath the rushing train, acutely aware of the blur of railroad ties just below his head. His steel-strong muscles were stretched to their utmost as he inched himself forward along the underbelly of the bulbous car.

"So where'd he go?" asked Sonny.

"Shut up and keep firing," ordered Hunger. They would get him eventually.

Seth had reached the end of the car and he swung himself up into the noisy little space between the two tank trucks. He rubbed his raw hands that had been cut up on his long tough climb toward safety. He rested there a moment, then poked his head out from the little cover he had. The firing had stopped but he distinctly heard the sounds of a dozen bike engines bursting into life as their riders savagely kick-started them.

Quickly Seth figured out what happened. The riders had hidden themselves in the trees by the side of the track and peppered the train with shot as it passed. The train rolled on, though, beyond them, and now they were racing to catch up with their prey.

Seth made his move. He jumped up onto the top of the tank car and sprinted along the tiny catwalk, running like hell for the cover of the engine and his trusty M3. He jumped onto the first car, then tumbled over the tall coal pile and fell onto the foot plate, safe.

Hunger watched his run for cover.

"Look," he screamed, "that black fuck ain't dead yet." He fed his big engine some more gas and in a swirl of gravel sped out onto the track. It was bumpy going for the Stormers as they charged over the wooden railway ties.

"I'm gonna break my fuckin' forks," screamed one.

Hunger realized the danger and pulled the force back onto the side of the track.

Seth slipped the leather strap of the M3 onto his shoulder as if to anchor it there, then he leaned out of the cab just as he thought the Stormers had forsaken the bone-shaking ride on the track for the easier path of the verge that ran next to the rusty iron highway. He swung the M3 and spat a dozen steel-jacketed slugs into the knot of riders that trailed him like vultures following a dying man in the desert. Seth exposed himself to their fire for only a second or two but he managed to take down two Stormers. Their bikes shot up the side of the embankment and crashed in the underbrush.

A high-pitched chorus of automatic weapons' fire whined around the cab, and bits of spiky, splintered coal whipped around him. Again Seth swung out, and his accurate, deadly fire was rewarded with the scalp of another Stormer. He could see clearly the top of the man's skull shear away and spin into the air like a hairy top.

Hunger saw another of his men fall and cursed at the top of his lungs, his oaths lost in the roar of his bikers. He had lost three men already and he couldn't afford to lose any more. But he would be damned if he was going to let the tough black man with a deadly trigger get away. . . .

He slowed up a little and his force obediently slowed too, although Sonny looked disgusted.

"You breaking off boss?" screamed Sonny. "We can take that shit!"

"Strategy," bellowed Hunger, and he tapped the side of his skull with a blue-black fingernail: *smarts*, he was saying.

Hunger pulled back and jumped in behind the train, riding on the ties again. The hell with the forks, he thought; if he brought down Seth, then Leather would reward them. His men jumped the rails and followed him. In seconds the entire force was tucked in the lee of the train, riding behind the last car. The ride was bumpy, too bone-jarring to even think of firing, but they were sheltered from Seth's sweeping fire. Seth saw them vanish behind him and he knew they were blocked about a hundred yards behind him. He smiled. That was just where he wanted them. . . .

He leaned out of the cab and looked down the track. A half mile ahead he saw exactly the kind of rail terrain he wanted. The tracks ran into a narrow culvert. There the rails had been laid through solid rock. The sheer sides of the cut ran almost straight up; the _gray rock stood at an incline that no bike could climb. Seth tugged up the throttle and picked up a little speed.

He entered the culvert and raced through it, the clatter of his engine echoing off the solid dead walls. It was a long piece of rock, maybe three hundred yards in length, and just as the lumbering train raced out of it and on into slightly more open country, Seth slammed on the brakes, locking them in place. The scream of iron on iron accused him stridently of abusing his iron mistress.

"Sorry, sugar," he whispered. The train was brought from speed to a halt in seconds, slid along the rails for a few yards, then stopped. Steam vented crazily from the stack and the thump-thump of the metal condenser echoed in the morning air.

"He stopped," screamed Hunger. "Now I'm going to _drill_ that fucking niggah. . . ."

The Stormers screamed along the track, heading

toward the stationary train, sure that Seth had broken down or given up or something: either way, they figured they had won and that Seth was as good as dead.

Seth listened to the wail of his pursuers' bikes bouncing off the tall rock walls of the culvert. He couldn't see them but he could tell by the steadily increasing sound more or less where they were in relation to the train. When he judged that they had passed the midway in the cut, Seth slammed the throttle up to full power and threw his giant engine into reverse. At first, the wheels just slipped on the track, as if complaining about the rough treatment that they were receiving at Seth's hands.

Then, somehow, the big wheels caught and the train began moving backward. Slowly at first, then, in a matter of seconds, the massive weight of the contraption and the sudden surge of power that Seth had bestowed on it fused, making the whole train gain speed suddenly. Seth's eyes were glued to the pressure gauge. He watched as the needle slowly climbed and the train picked up speed.

"Come on, come *on*," he mumbled.

At fifty yards he was moving again. The huge vessel was moving down the track, eating up the yards between it and the stunned raider force. After Seth had hit speed they realized the terrible beauty of his destructive plan. They were trapped.

"The crazy fuck is going to run us down," screamed Sonny.

The bulbous nose of the rearward car backed along the track toward them. The train filled the culvert from wall to wall. Suddenly the tough Stormers were caught in a frenzy of fear. They couldn't get around the train and they couldn't ride their bikes up the sheer walls of the cut. They had a good two-hundred-and-fifty-yard run to freedom if they were going to escape the inexorable weight of a terrible death. They were bunched together and tried to turn, but bikes got caught in other bikes, riders screamed and cursed, and all the while the massive bulk of the tank cars rolled toward them.

"Fuck! Fuck!" screamed Hunger.

Seth saved a piece of throttle for the last few yards separating his vast iron fist from the Stormers. Hot steam coursed into the cylinder, and like a muscle flexing, the train surged over the first of the fleeing Stormers. A rider glanced over his shoulder and saw a steel wall, as tall as a cliff behind him. The train showed no mercy, rolling over him, dragging the rider and his bike down as if the movement of the train was some kind of sucking tide. The heavy steel crushed him to a mash mixed in with the flattened pieces of the bike. Man and machine fused together, a fleshy metal mess on the rail bed.

The train slammed into a nest of riders and they screamed as merciless tons of cold steel rolled over them. They screamed until their throats and heads were crushed like unripe melons, popping on the rails with a flash of color and hair.

Hunger looked over his shoulder and saw that most of his force had vanished. The heavy chunking sound of the train on the track was coming closer, like a steel tidal wave building up behind him. The heavy rear buffer struck him mid-back and splintered his spine, pushing him down onto his bike. He could no longer control his machine or maintain his balance. The bike fell over and sprawled the Stormer across the rails. The massive steel wheels rolled over him, cutting through bone like wire cutters and slicing him into a half-dozen meaty chunks.

Seth jumped onto the coal pile and looked down the track. The Stormers were gone, all of them felled by the weight of the train. He slowed the reverse motion of the huge vehicle, came to a stop, then slowly brought his steel demoness forward. The wheels rolled over the fallen, again making them into an unrecognizable fleshy mush.

As he reentered the cut he saw a Stormer halfway up, clinging to the rocky side like a cat chased up a tree. The train lumbered by him at about thirty miles an hour. Seth squatted down on the foot plate, folded over his gun, and spat a few hot slugs into the madly scrabbling man. He flattened against the rock face and then, as life left him, he let go and bounded down the hard surface, his body thudding onto the empty tank car passing beneath him. The tank boomed dully as the man hit. He was sprawled there, his back arched over the top.

Seth checked the track ahead of him, set the throttle,

then strolled back to the middle car and kicked the dead man onto the open track. That done he lit another cigar and exhaled, content again—but this time a little watchful.

Chapter Fourteen

There wasn't a whole hell of a lot of Altoona left but it was in better shape than a lot of rubble towns Bonner had seen in his time on the road. The old mills that had once provided Altoona with its reason for being had been flattened as if by some giant, invisible, immensely powerful hand. Over the years the slaves had taken away sheets of corrugated iron to build crude shelters.

What had once been downtown was now just a few streets of shabby, weed-encrusted ruins. But Seth had chosen the site where they were to meet up for some very good reasons. He liked the old station there; he knew that the switches still worked and that the rail yards weren't jammed with rolling stock rusted fast to crumbling rails. Best of all, there was an old water tank with no top that usually filled up with rainwater. Filling the boiler of the locomotive with a bucket was a pain in the ass and it took up the better part of the day with back-breaking labor even for a man with Seth's strength and single-minded devotion to work.

Bonner and the rest of his force motored slowly through the shattered streets, their engines booming in the still, melancholy air.

"Where we s'posed to meet him?" asked Beck.

"At the old station."

"Makes sense."

They got to the ruined red-brick structure and found no sign of their comrade.

"So now what do we do?"

"We wait," said Bonner.

"How do we know he's coming?"

"He's coming."

"Fucking nigger," said Beck, "who needs him?"

"What a fucking dimwit you are," Starling said. "We need Seth bad."

"Oh yeah? How come?"

"Think about it asshole, how much gas can you carry on that bike of yours? Seth has three fucking tanker cars on the back of his goddamn loco. With that much room we can haul away enough gas to make us all rich. That's why we need Seth."

"Oh," said Beck. He paused a moment. "You know, I heard that Leather was going to put tax men in this shithole of a town."

"No sign of them," said Bonner.

"Well, if it's all the same to you guys, I'm gonna walk around and take me a little look-see. I don't want no surprises. I hate surprises, you know what I mean?"

"Be my guest."

Beck shouldered his big machine gun and ambled off slowly down the street. He knew that he was unlikely to find anything of value in the ruins—this area had been stripped a long time ago—but he was glad he was going alone, just in case he happened on some loot that he could claim as his own.

The rest of the party sat silently in their vehicles or on the chipped steps of the station. As the hours passed, the Habs took out some dice and started a quiet gambling game among themselves.

Bonner found himself a patch of sun and dozed, listening to the sound of the light wind moaning through the broken buildings and the rattle of the dice and the quiet curses and exclamations of the northmen. The Mean Brothers found a scrawny kitten, its thin rib bones protruding through its dirty fur, and they played with the tiny animal, gently petting it with their vast hands.

Hours passed and Bonner slept, although he wakened immediately when his subconscious sensed Beck's return, picking up the heavy tread of his boots in the broken street. The giant raider walked up to Bonner and stood over him. Bonner opened his eyes and sheilded them with his hand from the sun that glowed over Beck's burly shoulder.

"There's something down the road a piece that I think you should see."

"What?"

"And spoil the surprise?" said Beck. "Come on."

Bonner, Starling, and J.B. followed Beck through the bombed-out streets. No one spoke. They could smell their objective long before they could see it. Bonner shut his eyes for a second. He knew the smell well: death.

At what seemed to be the center of the old town a crude gallows had been erected. Hanging from it were two naked bodies some two or three days dead. And it was plain that these two men, whoever they had been, had died in great agony. They were hung by meat hooks that had been jammed into the soft flesh under their chins, their weight resting on their big jaw bones. The points of the hooks poked through the tongues and mouths. Their tongues and lips were black. Their eyes had been burned out. As the riders looked, a fat torpid fly emerged from one of the torn mouths and hummed along the putrefying flesh of the man's chest. The two mutilated corpses swung slowly in the cold breeze.

"Them Stormers don't fool around, do they?" said Beck. "What do you s'pose these two slaves did to piss 'em off so much?"

"*Sacre bleu*," said J.B., unable to tear his horrified gaze off the two dead men. "They are very bad men these Stormers, I think."

Bonner stepped back from the twisted corpses. A

huge pool of blood dried black lay beneath the carcasses.

"They're not slaves," he said.

"How can you tell?"

"They're too well fed. They have flesh on their bones."

"Then they ain't Stormers," said Beck. "Stormers never travel in twos. And they don't look like no riders I ever seen. Of course, how the fuck can you tell what they looked like."

"No," said Bonner, "they aren't riders. They're the tax men you said Leather was putting in here. Slave revolt. That's what happened here."

Starling looked at the naked bodies. There were crusty red holes where the tax men's genitals had been. "Man, them slaves really hold a grudge."

As he spoke, a voice hot and heavy with hate screamed into the cold air.

"Death to Stormers!" There was the dull boom of a shotgun and a shower of rocks. Whoever held the firearm was not used to using it, for the shells dug up the pavement yards from where the riders stood.

"Holy shit," said Starling as the stones bounced around him. The riders scattered, darting into the safety of a ruin. All the men pulled their guns except Bonner.

"Those fucks," bellowed Beck. "Those fucking slaves! They fired at us. They think we're fucking Stormers. Where are they? Let me see one and I'll fucking blow him to pieces."

Another wave of stones scattered at their feet. "I'm going to fucking slice them!" Beck screamed.

"They're only slaves," said Bonner. "They can't hurt us."

"One of 'em has a gun," put in Starling.

"But he has no idea how to use it right," said J.B.

"Let's get back to the station," said Bonner. The four men darted through the streets, running from doorway to doorway, rocks and glass dogging their hurried footsteps.

The Habs and the Mean Brothers had come under fire too from another band of slaves. When the four men returned from their own encounter, a Canadian jabbered at J.B., pointing across the street.

"He says they are on that roof there."

"Which roof where, Frenchy?" demanded Beck.

"That one." J.B. pointed to the upper story of a broken building that faced the station.

"Good," said Beck.

"Beck," said Bonner, "leave them. You could kill 'em all if you wanted, but why bother?"

"I want to. They think I'm a fucking Stormer. No one calls me a Stormer."

As if sensing Beck's anger and attempting to add to it, a voice rang out. "Give up, Stormers, we got you surrounded."

"The fuck you do," screamed Beck, "and we ain't Stormers!"

"No tricks," replied the voice. "Come out before we kill you all."

"How do you like the balls of that guy?" said Beck. "All they got is rocks."

With that the gun boomed again, splintering a doorframe next to Beck. A splinter shot into his arm and quivered there, stuck in his flesh. Beck pulled it out. "Okay, Bonner, they made me mad. Now they get it."

Beck kicked open the door and a hail of rocks bounced around him. One struck him painfully in the knee. He hopped around in pain on the steps, bellowing inarticulate screams of pain and anger. "Okay, you fucks, you asked for it." He hopped down the steps; when the gun fired again, he scarcely noticed the chunk of pavement it tore up.

Beck pulled a heavy Thompson 27A machine gun and chunked the drum magazine into the slot. "Bye slaves," exclaimed the giant, and let fly.

The big .45-caliber bullets tore up the low parapet that shielded the eight or nine thin, weak men. Bullets flew into their bodies and they fell with a scream. When Beck used up his thirty-shot clip, he rooted around in the saddlebag of his bike, found another, fit it to the stock, and fired again. There were no more rocks, no more shotgun shells. "Okay," he shouted, "satisfied now?"

There was no answer.

"You didn't have to get sliced, you know," Beck shouted. "Fucking fools." He tossed the gun back into the bag and rejoined the rest of the party. His sleeve was damp with the blood from the wound raised by the splinter.

Bonner looked disgustedly at him. "How many did you get?"

"How the fuck should I know?" Beck slumped to the ground and lay there in moody silence for the next few hours. He didn't even rouse himself when Seth slowly steamed into the station.

Bonner greeted his friend warmly. "Any trouble on the rails?"

"Some Stormers, nothing special. You have any hot spots."

"A couple. Look, we gotta get moving. Leather has taken over this spot but there's been a revolt. I figure it won't be long before they send some Stormers out to check on this place. No sense in waiting for them."

"Yeah," put in Starling, "it's getting cold too. I wanna find that gas and get back to Chicago."

"I just gotta fill up with water, then I'm ready to move. You guys got any idea where this gas is."

"Further south is how I figure it. You know the rails down that way?" asked Bonner.

"Know them well," said Seth. Then he caught sight of Beck and smiled. "Hey Beck, my man . . ."

"What took you so fucking long?" growled Beck.

"What's bothering him?" asked Seth puzzled.

"Bad mood," said Starling.

The lone slave who had survived Beck's quick raking fire lay on the roof of the old building for hours. He watched the blood drain out of the men slain around him and wondered how he had got mixed up in this whole thing. They never should have killed the tax soldiers . . . but when they had beaten Louisa to death . . . it had been too much for them to stand. The men had acted without thinking, grabbing the tax men and killing them in the most gruesome way they knew how. It had felt good, but now this other group of men had come along and one man killed a dozen slaves. It had all been a terrible mistake.

He heard the men across the streets talking, and they seemed to stay for hours while they worked on the huge thing that had come rolling into town spitting smoke and fire. He was cramped and cold and scared, but he knew what he was going to do. As soon as the men left he was going to run, he didn't know where but he had to get out of this place. Two tax men dead meant that there were more Stormers coming and that meant more death. Probably his.

Along about nightfall he heard the engines of the riders burst into life. They rolled out of town, following one of the vehicles that had a bright light attached to the front. When the sound of their engines died away, he crawled from his hiding place and fled.

Chapter Fifteen

Leatherman traveled in style. Trailing behind his Radlep battalion were a half-dozen trucks, each filled to the backboards with food and liquor and girls, so that even when he was on the road, the president of the Slavestates managed to avoid roughing it. He figured that there was no point living in shit when he didn't have to: any damn-fool fuck-up could be uncomfortable. He was the Leatherman after all, and he had worked hard and done a lot of messy killing to get where he was today. And after having done all that hard work, he was going to make the most of it.

His huge convoy had camped down for the night in the parking lot of a big old shopping center somewhere on the outskirts of the old mill towns. Leather didn't really know the name of the place and he couldn't have cared less. The low dark ruins of the mall were just like a thousand others he had seen: they always looked as if they had been drenched in broken glass. A few cracked signs identified the old stores: Fayva, Pantry Pride, Radio Shack, Zalduondo's Bakery De-Lites, Baskin Robbins . . . Leather didn't care about those places either.

As soon as the convoy stopped, servant slaves were put to work making up the campsite. A fire was started from wood cut from some stunted trees that had forced themselves up through the cracks in the asphalt, and it was fed with larger pieces of wood that the servants gathered from the roadside and the shell of the shattered shopping center. Once the blaze was going they began preparing the pig—pork was Leather's favorite meat—for roasting.

A second group of slaves set to work erecting Leather's tent. It was a large one, big enough for a fluffy double bed that was carried so that their leader could always sleep in comfort. Soon after the bed was made up a couple of slave women, carefully chosen from Leather's harem, would climb in and wait there until Leather was finished eating and drinking with his men around the campfire.

The Radleps didn't sleep under canvas, a lot of them didn't sleep at all: they were often kept awake through the night by the pain of their terrible disease. They would curl up next to their bikes, and if they could, they slept; if not, they ignored the bitter cold and the snow that whipped around their huddled forms. None of the Radleps slept heavily, not because of the discomfort but simply because alertness was part of their training. Leather had seen a Radlep squad leap out of bed as awake and taut as if they had done speed—all in a matter of seconds. Even so, a large number of the 'leps would be placed on watch. They would stand on the perimeter of the camp, their weapons at the ready, silent and attuned to every sound and every tiny movement in the icy night. They would wait and watch, ready at any moment to kill and die in defense of their evil leader. Unlike Stormers and other normal men, the Radleps didn't talk or laugh or stamp their feet to keep themselves warm or even quietly curse the cold. They just watched and brooded, silent as human tombstones. . . .

But before the battalion settled in for the long night there was a good deal of eating and drinking to do. Before too long the smell of roast pig quietly wafted through the snowy air and men licked their raw, torn lips and looked forward to the feast to come.

Leather always started these things off. A fat, overstuffed armchair, the kind that people used to have in their living rooms, would be brought from one of the supply trucks, and Leather would settle in it close to the fire. The rest of the company, squatting on the cold asphalt, 'leps and Stormers and other functionaries, made a circle around the fire.

Beyond the warmth of the roaring fire but just caught in the outermost rays of orange light lurked the servant slaves, a few of the Radleps' whores and the cook slaves, standing there nervously until summoned by their masters.

The business of eating would go on for hours. Radleps would eat their fill then steal away into the night to relieve their comrades that stood watch on the cold perimeter. There was little conversation, although occasionally Leather, comfortable in his armchair, a piece of pork impaled on the blade of his left hand, would make some observation with which everyone would agree or crack a joke at which everyone would laugh uproariously. Mostly, though, Leather just ate, quickly and noisily, cramming as much food into his mouth as it could take while clear rivers of pig fat smeared across his face and ran down his hairy arms. A slave girl would clean it off his body once he was asleep.

Leather's manners were good compared to the 'leps. Watching a group of them eat was enough to turn the stomach of a hardened, battle-weary Stormer. Food would get chewed up by brown teeth, then little bits of the mush would course from broken cheeks or out through bleeding lips. They grunted and chewed and held the greasy meat in scaly hands, unaware that they were pictures of grotesque disgust. Had they known, they wouldn't have cared. Leather never seemed to notice. But then, everybody knew he was crazy about his radiation lepers.

The meal was almost over when Carlos the Radlep commander limped to where Leather sat and interrupted his leader as he slurped up a piece of pig fat while absently fondling the breast of a slave girl who kneeled by the side of the armchair. Carlos whispered in Leatherman's ear.

"No shit," Leatherman said after hearing the message. "Bring the fuck here. Lemme see him."

A few Radleps looked up from their greasy dinners like dogs from the feeding bowl. What was up, they wondered.

With a short snap of his head, Carlos gestured toward someone in the darkness and out of the gloom came a Radlep clutching a terrified-looking slave on his large cracked hand. The force with which he held the man had caused the thin delicate burned skin of the Radlep's hand to part and tear, and thin watery blood flowed from the wide lesions. The liquid dribbled down onto the thin shift that the slave wore.

Leather stopped gnawing on a piece of meat that was stuck on one of his knife hands long enough to stare at his captive. He glanced at the man without interest. He was just another colorless, pale, thin, malnourished slave who didn't know it, but he didn't have much time to live. He was just a tiny piece in Leather's empire.

"So, who are you, you piece of shit?" Leather spoke as if the whole thing rather bored him.

"We found him out by the perimeter," wheezed Carlos. The 'lep commander's voice box was going, and speaking was difficult for him. Each breath he took, each word he spoke caused a little bit of his tortured throat to crack. He tasted blood in his mouth constantly. "What were you doing out there, dogshit?" rasped Carlos. "Tell the man."

Leather crammed some more food into his mouth and chewed noisily. The slave—it was the man who had escaped Beck's dangerous performance with the sub-machine gun—couldn't speak. In truth, it had been the sight of the fire and the tantalizing smell of roasting meat that had brought him so close to the camp. He had never smelled anything so delicious in his life. Sometimes in the past he had crept close to the tax soldiers' house in the town and smelled the cooking there, but even they had never had anything that had an odor so intoxicatingly wonderful. The slave's mouth opened and closed a few times and he stared at Leatherman, but fear and cold and hunger prevented him from managing a single coherent word.

Without really thinking about it, the Radlep who had caught the slave stuffed the butt of his M16 into the lower back of the slave. The sudden, short, painful blow sent the thin man to his knees. He knelt on the asphalt, skinning his knees as he fell, and retched and wheezed from the force of the blow.

"Speak when you're spoke to," ordered Carlos.

"Where you from?" asked Leather.

"Down the road," stuttered the slave, finally finding his tongue.

"Where down the road?"

"Al-al-Altoona . . ."

"What's your name?"

"S-S-Stanley . . ."

"Okay, Stanley my man," said Leather affably, "you know who I am?"

Stanley looked around at the Radleps, the women,

the food, and then into Leather's single cruel blue
eye. "Are you G-G-God?"

Leather threw his head back and laughed heartily.
Because he laughed, his force laughed with him.

"Hey Stanley," said Leatherman, "you see that?"
He gestured toward a big Beretta-686 shotgun clasped
by a Radlep.

The slave nodded.

"You know what that is?"

Stanley nodded again. He sure knew what it was.
He had seen a dozen slaves, maybe more, die by the
gun. Not just at Beck's hands; he had seen slaves
killed by Stormers, and the tax men were always
knocking off one or two just for the hell of it.

"Yeah," said Leather, "what is it?"

"A g-g-gun."

"You're right. That's God, Stanley. A gun makes
you a god. And I got more guns than anybody else.
So I guess you've guessed right. I am God." Leather
roared with laughter again. He liked this little slave.
He had never thought of things that way before.
Sure, Leather thought, he had no problem at all
thinking he was God. "Say, Carlos, how far are we
from Altoona?"

"Not that far. Maybe twenty miles."

"That's pretty far for a slave, ain't it?"

"That's right."

"What you doing so far from home, Stanley?"

Stanley's heart sank. What could he say? That the
slaves had had enough? That they had risen up against
the tax men and killed and tortured them, the way

they had beat, abused, raped, and killed the slaves all these years? And why didn't this man know already? Surely it was he who had sent the men with the guns. Surely this man was so powerful that he had a man so strong that he could kill all the slaves with one burst of fire.

Stanley was mute.

"So how 'bout it, Stanley?"

The Radlep behind him raised the stock of his weapon threateningly. Stanley knew that he couldn't take another blow.

"I ran away," he said in a very small voice.

"That's bad, Stanley," said Leather.

"I'm sorry," Stanley whimpered. "But everyone has been punished."

"Punished?" said Leather, puzzled. "Punished for what?"

"For the revolt."

Leather's body seemed to quiver suddenly with rage. His ugly face turned a livid red. "Revolt."

Stanley nodded. "But they are all dead now. You killed them all, except me."

"The fuck I did!" yelled Leather. "Who revolted? What happened? Who punished you?"

Slowly, haltingly, Stanley told the story of the revolt, of the death of the tax men, of the sudden arrival of the men that Stanley and the other slaves took to be Stormers.

"A man shot them?"

"That's right."

"They weren't Stormers, Stanley. Because if they

had been Stormers, they would have done more than shoot you revolting motherfuckers. Man, they would have . . .'' Leather gasped for words. ''Man, you woulda paid bad. Now tell me about the fuck that did the shooting.''

Stanley had only caught a short glimpse of Beck but he told what he knew. He was the largest man he had ever seen and he had friends; they came in cars and trucks and one was on a bike. . . . Then a man had come on a . . . He didn't know what to call Seth's locomotive but he described it as best he could.

Leather listened, then spoke slowly, his teeth clenched: ''Beck, Bonner, Starling, Seth . . . The same little crew that gave us headaches last time.''

''And they're in Altoona,'' said Carlos.

''Or pretty damn close. Strike the camp. We're going now. Send the dog men out ahead. Now.''

''Yes, boss,'' said Carlos, and he marched away, painfully bellowing orders as he went.

''Now you, Stanley, are lucky we ain't got much time. Cause if we had, I would have seen that you got all the pain that your dead friends didn't get. As it is, I'm pressed for time. Take him, Sammy.''

Stanley was hustled away and given a quick piece of Radlep torture. He was strung up by the wrists, his thin body hoisted up into the air by means of a rope thrown over a tall yellow plastic arch that stood in front of a low glass and wood building in the middle of the shopping mall parking lot. A smashed sign stood off to one side: OVER 110 BILLION . . .

Stanley wailed with the pain and fear that pumped

through his body and he arched his scrawny neck to look below his dangling feet. Servants and Radleps were building a fire underneath him.

The dog men were leaving as the first wave of heat wafted up to his naked feet, singeing the hair on his frail legs.

By the time the camp was struck and the Radleps and their leader were moving off into the night, Stanley's skin had charred and flaked and the smell of his burned flesh mingled with the odor of the burned carcass of the pig that no one had thought to remove from the roasting fire.

The column left and Stanley's tortured screams tore through the empty night.

Chapter Sixteen

The dog men were Leather's trackers and he always made sure that a few of them were carried along when he went on the road. The dog men moved fast enough to be sent out ahead of the column like the Radlep scouts, but they carried a little extra, an edge that made them feared and hated—but very good at what they did.

Before the camp was even half dismantled and long before Stanley's pathetic wails rang out in the night, the dog men were off and running. They bucketed out onto the road, put their heads down, and headed for Altoona.

They were a funny breed, these guys, and they tended to stick together, preferring the company of other dog men or best of all, their great, muscled dogs. Leather dispatched all three of his trackers and they pounded down the road with Leather's orders ringing in their ears: *find him*.

They were mounted on three-wheeled motorcycles, great hunks of iron that were mostly homemade out of a dozen pieces of a dozen other bikes. The machines bounced along on three large all-terrain tires that were the special gift of the Leatherman. Each man was heavily armed, of course, but each knew that his most effective weapon was not his hardware but the massive dog that rode in the cages built high in the back of the trike, just behind the rider's back.

Inside each cage squatted a dog of immense size and of a breed that would have been unrecognizable to the citizens of an older age, when dogs had been kept around the house to have their ears pulled by young children and to do tricks. No, these animals were something else altogether: they were part mastiff, part pit bull, part wild. They were a couple hundred pounds of bone and muscle whose only purpose was to serve the demands of a powerful set of jaws and twin rows of razor-sharp teeth.

The dog men were from the south and these dogs had been bred and taught in tough swamp country by men who didn't quite fit into the mold of the new world. The massive short-haired brown dogs seemed to share their masters' taste for the kill, for blood.

As soon as the motorcycles roared out onto the dark cold highway, a peculiar animal fury seemed to rise in animal and rider alike. As the dog men crouched low over their handlebars, noses into the wind almost

as if they sensed blood on the icy air, so the dogs
crouched forward in their cages, growling at the
rushing air as if they knew that every inch of highway they covered brought them closer to the ecstasy
of a kill.

The icy miles passed quickly and as a gray dawn
broke over a frozen landscape the dog men charged
into the quiet ruins of the ghost town. The three
machines screeched to a halt in the middle of the
main street, where night shadows still seemed to
lurk.

The leader of the small squad swung off his machine and took a few steps down the street, his eyes
alive; he appeared to be sniffing the air. His fellow
riders sat still in their saddles, but the dogs scratched
and whined as if they were anxious for the bloodlet-
ting that was to come.

"Well," said the leader, "they been here all right."

"How do you know?" asked one of the riders.

"Little feeling I got."

The two mounted men nodded. That was all the
explanation they needed.

"Now," said the leader, "which way did they
go . . . ?"

"Reckon we can find out."

"Reckon we can," said the leader softly, "reckon
we can." He walked slowly to his caged animal, the
dog bounding against the heavy metal wire, delirious
with joy as she realized that her master was about to
set her free. The man slid back the heavy bolt that
secured the door and the dog, knowing the routine,

lay down on the floor of her cage whimpering. The dog man threw the door wide open, giving the beast a tantalizing glimpse of freedom. The master grabbed the dog's mammoth head between his rough hands and whispered in her ear: "Now come on now," he said softly. "You come on and make your daddy proud, you hear?"

The huge beast bounded from her confines, prancing on the road at her master's side. The other two dogs, jealous of the freedom of their mate, set up a terrible barking and growling.

"Quiet there," shouted one of the riders, "you'll get your chance."

The soft sensitive snout of the freed dog bent to the cracked road and the animal moved around in a few wide crooked circles, then, like an arrow, seemed to lock on a scent. The handler rapped out a command: "Go, girl."

The dog sprang forward, the powerful muscles in her shoulders and hindquarters propelling her along the street like a torpedo. Deep in her throat a growl of pure animal blood lust was born, and as she ran, it developed into a harsh, full-throated, ferocious howl.

The handler watched the dog dash across the street, hot on the scent of something. She skidded at the entrance of a broken building and wailed. A man broke from his cover within and dashed down the street, the dog hard on his heels.

The man glanced over his shoulder, saw the bared teeth of the animal, and screamed, his wild cries seeming to tear a groove in the morning air. The slave ran, his heart pumping in his thin chest. A scrawny tree that had once given shade to the street was right in his path and he clawed his way up the naked trunk, grabbed the lowest branch, and was just about to swing himself up to safety when the dog leaped high in the air and clamped down with her steel-trap jaws on the dangling foot of the petrified slave.

The sharp incisors sliced down deep into the bony foot and the jaws locked. The dog hung there, pulling at her prey with all her weight. Blood poured down onto her nose, threatening to drown her. She snuffed to clear her nostrils of gore, refusing to let go.

The other two dogs had been released and they were dancing around under the screaming man, jumping up, their jaws snapping like traps.

The dog men wandered over nonchalantly and stood under the tortured man. All three men thrust their hands into the back pockets of their pants and watched for a moment.

Finally the leader spoke. "You gonna be good, boy?"

"Call it off! Call it off!" screamed the slave.

"You gonna behave?"

The slave nodded, his eyes wide with pain and fear.

"Down, girl," shouted the chief. The dog unclamped her teeth, dropped to the ground, and sat obediently. The other two dogs stopped barking and lay down.

"Come on down, boy."

The slave let go and dropped to the ground, landing painfully on his chewed-up foot. He yelped as he hit the pavement and grabbed at the bloody wound as if trying to squeeze out the pain. The dogs growled as he writhed; he never took his terrified eyes off them.

"Now," said the lead handler, "where did they go?"

"Who?"

One of the assistants kicked the mangled foot savagely and the slave wailed again. He placed his boot under the nose of one of the dogs, who gratefully licked the tasty warm blood off the toe.

The leader looked down at the slave and rubbed his whiskers. "Now don't you be that way, boy, or these little ladies here are going to tear you apart. Now a couple of days ago there were some boys here and I heard that they gave the folks here some trouble. You tell us where they went and we'll go see that they never bother you again."

The slave seemed to trust them. He spoke slowly. "They headed out of town. They took the road that way. . . ." He gestured.

"And when was this?"

"Yesterday."

"Good boy," said the leader, as if he was praising one of his dogs. "Now that wasn't so bad, was it? We're going to be on our way now. Sorry about the foot."

The slave relaxed a little.

"C'mere, girl," said the leader, and the first dog

jumped up and trotted happily to her master's side and licked the handler's long thin hand. The man fondled the heavy fur on the dog's neck for a moment.

"Dang," he said, "almost forgot."

"Forgot what?" said the slave. He didn't notice that the other two handlers were smiling broadly.

"Why I almost forgot that it's just about *feeding time*."

The dogs heard the magic words, and with a yelp they fell upon the slave. The long teeth slashed into the man's thin body. The bone razors set in their jaws tore the man into a red raw mess of muscles and meat.

The slave summoned up every ounce of strength that remained in his frail form and thrashed violently in a vain attempt to throw off the devouring beasts.

The jaws squeezed shut, cracking a narrow bone in his arm. A dog latched on to an ear, dug her forelegs into the ground, and pulled and shook her head at the same time until the thin flesh and cartilage gave way. The dog fell back into a heap on her hindquarters, gobbling up the ear like a bloody mushroom. The third dog burrowed into the soft flesh of the groin and tore back and forth like a threshing machine.

The handlers watched as their beasts quickly pulled the slave to pieces. When they judged that the dogs had eaten enough to keep them alive but not so much that they would lose their appetites for further killing, they called them off. The brainwashed animals stopped their anxious snarling and chewing immediately and trotted to their masters' sides, licking their bloody, saliva-damp chops.

"Okay," said the leader, "let's go." The dogs jumped into their cages and the three motorcycles bumped away, leaving the gore-strewn body of the slave behind them.

Chapter Seventeen

Starling was asleep, so was Beck. J.B. and Les Habitants were all curled up in, on, under, or around their trucks. The Mean Brothers dozed somewhere on the outer edge of the circle.

Bonner was awake. He sat absolutely still, his back straight against the trunk of a pine tree. The frozen ground was cold on his legs and the back of the tree was hard and uncomfortable against his back. He was away from the dying embers of the fire; he preferred to stay away from the life-giving warmth for fear it would edge him down the road toward sleep and because the friendly light could show his position, bringing a sudden death down on him and his small force.

There was danger around, every fiber of his body

reacted, telling him that somewhere out there lurked a menace waiting for its chance to strike.

About an hour before he had heard, far off, the whine of motorcycles. He listened intently, like a cat, and had managed to determine that there were not that many in the force that was traveling the roads that late winter's night. No more than five, for sure. Bonner turned over all the possibilities in his mind: riders from Chi? Unlikely . . . A small group of Radlep scouts? Maybe, but the scouts usually worked in pairs and he had definitely heard more than two bikes. A small party of Stormers? Bonner couldn't remember the last time he had heard of a group of Stormers traveling in a group that small. Dog men—maybe. They were just Leather's speed. Yeah, thought Bonner, 'leps or dog men.

But the sounds of the bikes were long gone now. Of course, he told himself, that didn't mean much. The big blue night may have swallowed up the sounds but that didn't mean that the riders weren't around someplace. A heavy wave of fatigue—it seemed almost thick and viscous, like honey—began creeping over him and, involuntarily, Bonner relaxed for a moment.

He stared up through the overhanging branches of the trees and found he could just catch a glimpse of the the sky and the bright spangle of winter stars. They were so far off, so clean, so peaceful looking, so removed from the death and dirt that was Bonner's world. . . . He wondered idly if there was another place, a happier planet where history had not derailed itself, where men had not made the mistakes that had plunged the earth into cruelty and hate. . . .

A footfall in the soft carpet of the forest floor pulled Bonner back to the night that suddenly seemed to stretch before him like a black desert. He cursed himself for getting lazy, for believing, if only for a moment, that he could remove himself from the constant danger of his world by dreaming about another.

He shook himself. Now, he asked himself, had he heard a footstep or not? Bonner's mind ran back over the sound as he tried to recall exactly what he had heard. He decided that he had in fact heard a footstep. The shotgun slid from its leather holster like a deadly steel snake. The Steyr lay across his knees. He moved it and quietly rose into a crouch, sure that the crack of his stiff knee could be heard throughout the forest.

The tiredness was gone and his senses were alive. There was someone—something—there in the darkness, and Bonner's total mind and strength were now committed to the struggle of destroying it before it destroyed him.

Bonner was not prepared for what happened next. He thought he heard the faintest whisper, no more than a swish of breath between lips. It was followed a second later by a heavy, colossal living weight that came flying out of the night to bring him down. The total surprise of the attack caught him off guard and he fell to the ground with a heavy thud, the heavy animal on top of him all claws and teeth and a deafening hideous growling filling his ear.

Bonner wrestled the beast for a second but could

feel the deep animal determination as the dog's teeth snapped and snarled, tearing at his clothes, frantically searching for flesh. Bonner jammed his fist into the warm mouth, losing a strip of flesh as he pushed his powerful hand through the curtain of teeth. The animal writhed and Bonner could feel the saliva of the beast mixing with the sweet blood that flowed from his hand. The taste seemed to inflame the animal and she kicked and growled and snorted, trying to free the constriction in her throat so she could sink her teeth deep into Bonner's body.

He could feel the animal convulse and gag as the windpipe opened and closed, attempting to flex out the intrusion. Bonner clawed a bloody track on the inside of the mouth, feeling his nails scratch up a long skein of flesh.

Then the weight of a second dog landed on him, followed by a third. Bonner kicked his feet wildly, hoping that he would get lucky and his boot would find some part of the two savage beasts that would hurt them, slow them down, anything to keep those teeth from scything into his flesh. His foot connected with something and a dog yelped and fell away but the other one was luckier. It lunged at Bonner's legs and the teeth cut deep into his leg. He felt a sting as blood soaked his pants, cooling instantly in the cold air. The night was filled with the strangled gurglings of the dog that Bonner held in his grasp and the savage tearing growls of the other two.

Suddenly a dog was yanked off his body and Bonner took that moment of freedom to flip over, flattening the dog in whose throat his fist still was buried. He looked up to see a Mean Brother holding a dog by by the scruff of its neck as if it was a mere puppy. The Mean twisted the dog's face around and with the heel of his hand slammed against the hound's sensitive snout. There was a sharp snap like the sound of dry timber cracking as the shaft of the bone supporting the dog's long nose snapped. A mighty shove from the Mean drove the sharp sliver of bone backward, sliding deep into the animal brain, tearing the soft mushy organ to shreds. The dog died instantly.

Bonner had pulled his arm from the jaws of the animal and jammed the short barrel of his shotgun through the rows of teeth in its place. He felt the broken incisors clamp down on the steel. He pulled both triggers and the dog's head and neck vanished as if it was a bloody wet firecracker. The second Mean Brother had gotten hold of the third dog, thrown the wriggling beast to the ground, and squashed the furry throat with a crunch of his huge foot.

"You motherfuckers," screamed an anguished voice from the darkness.

The voice was torn and grief-stricken, creased and sorrowful with tears. It was one of the handlers. He had just witnessed the quick and violent death of a dog that he had set on a thousand men—usually defenseless, scared, weak men—and had always seen those bloody jaws emerge from human flesh with a lick and grin of victory.

The hate in the voice was backed with a tear of

9mm fire, ripping through the trees. Bonner and the Means dropped to the earth as bullets chewed up the ground around them. Bonner caught sight of the muzzle flash and he sprayed the area with the Steyr. A grunt echoed in the darkness followed by the heavy thud of a dead man falling. One, thought Bonner. He looked around him. The Mean Brothers had disappeared.

A shriek rang out in the night and Bonner knew instantly where the Means had vanished to. One or the other of the Means had taken another life with his bare hands.

Bonner listened a moment. Someone was running away, crashing through the underbrush, a defeated man. Without hesitation Bonner took off after him, pounding through the forest in hot pursuit. He ran a hundred yards or so, then dashed into some open ground, a clearing that was littered with the flat stumps of trees, suggesting that some logging had once been done in those parts. There, ahead of him, was the back of the fleeing dog handler. Bonner stopped, raised his light little wasp gun, and fired. A slash of bullets sprayed across the man's shoulders, and the force of the little bullets coupled with the speed of his run threw the dog man face-first on the ground. His lungs deflated and slowly began to fill with blood and fluid. In a minute or two he was dead, drowned in his own body juices.

The pain of his dog bite, irritated by the short, vigorous run through the woods, was beginning to bother Bonner. The violent struggle with the incredibly strong animal had tired him. He wanted to limp back to the camp, turn over the watch to Starling or Beck or Les Habs, and sleep for a few hours. He deserved it.

Starling and Beck stood in front of the fire, looking down with interest at the carcasses of the huge dogs.

"Fucking big," observed Starling.

"Haw," laughed Beck. "Still just a dog. I woulda wet myself laughing if that thing had gotten the big man Bonner hisself." He looked at Bonner and laughed again. "You dumb fuck, you almost got sliced by a *dog*."

Chapter Eighteen

Vidor smiled his ugly smile and looked around him at the dirty but happy faces of his Stormers.

"Well, boys," he said, "we done it."

"Damn right!" bellowed Sickert, his second in command, "Damn right we did."

Secretly, Vidor couldn't quite believe that they had done it. He looked around at the gooney faces of his men and told himself that they were one dumb collection of Stormers. And what more everybody knew it. In the Cap they said that Vidor's troop was the sorriest outfit in the entire Stormer brigade, bar none. But they had done it.

Leather had sent them out weeks ago and they had spent most of their time blundering around in the snow, falling over other patrols and even lying low once when they saw that big snowman force coming. That had been close.

They had run out of food twice and gas once and they had to raid some poor half-dead slaves to get something to eat. They had been forced to beg gas from another Stormer patrol. The other Stormers had looked down their noses at Vidor and his party, contempt showing plainly on their faces.

But those other jokers hadn't found it—Vidor and his skaggy men had. Now all they had to do was link up with the Leatherman and let him know of their find. Then they were home free—rich and heroes in the bargain. Vidor couldn't believe it.

"Men," he said, his voice cracking slightly, "I'm fuckin' proud of you. . . ."

Not one of the twenty bike men could believe his good fortune. They looked around them at the rusty gray bulks of the giant fuel tanks. There must have been at least a dozen of the rusting giant pods, all of them huddled together in a dirty, fenced-in old industrial park that sat in the middle of a deep cleft, a valley that seemed to be filled with acre upon acre of dead old factories and mills. An oily stream wandered down the middle of the valley as if it was lost, the water black and sluggish. The banks were choked with ancient garbage, as if the factories were still churning out whatever had been made there once upon a time.

Vidor was already busy making up a story about how he had had a hunch about where to look for the place, but the truth of it was that he and his little band of not-so-tough guys had gotten all turned around in a snowstorm a couple of days back. They ended up wandering into their find because by mistake they took a ruined, rarely traveled road out of Johnstown (hell, Vidor wasn't even sure that pile of ruins had been Johnstown. They all looked the same to him) on the Bethlehem side of Altoona (he thought) and they found it there, waiting for the first riders that happened along.

The tanks towered above them like rusty, snub-headed mountain peaks. Each of them had a rickety rusty metal staircase running up the side, skirting four-foot-high letters that were still readable under years of corrosion and faded by exposure to the sun and the rain: EXXON.

But none of the Stormers could read, not even Vidor, so they stared uncomprehendingly at the letters.

"What do it say?" one of them asked.

"Gasoline," said Vidor confidently. And if it didn't, it oughta, he thought.

"Makes sense," said Sickert.

There it was, the whole damn thing, thought Vidor. It was a vast inland sea of gasoline, a place that every rider, raider, gas hound, Stormer, and 'lep was looking for. Even Leather himself was looking for it. Right then, Vidor realized, he was the most powerful man on the continent. More powerful than Leather even. A very dim light began to shine in the back of his head and he looked a little dazed for a minute. He was thinking.

"You know," he said, fingering the stubble on his grimy chin, "you know what I'm thinking?"

"What?" asked Sickert.

"I'm thinking we are sitting on the biggest load of gas in the whole fuckin' Slavestates."

"Yeah, great, ain't it?" said Sickert happily.

"Yeah," said Vidor, speaking to the whole group, "but what do you say we do a little thinking on it before we go running to tell the Leatherman what we found here."

"But Leather . . ." began Sickert.

"Well, hell," said a Stormer named Dougal, "why should we give all this to Leather? We found it. It's ours."

"Right," said Vidor, "maybe Dougal gotta point."

The Stormers shifted uneasily. They all thought they deserved a little something for finding the gas, but the idea of taking on Leatherman . . . well, that seemed a little unreasonable.

"Are you crazy?" demanded Sickert. Never again in his life would he speak so forcefully or think so clearly. "Are you guys out of your minds? *We're* gonna take on *Leather*? The man is not in the Cap. The man is on the road and he's got a whole 'lep battalion with him. If you think some fuck-ups like us are gonna do any damage against him, then you dumb and you crazy too."

"Shut up, Sickert," yelled Vidor.

"The hell I will. You're making a big mistake. I say take the news to Leatherman and he'll do the right thing for us. If you don't, then you're gonna end up dead. Kilt.''

Vidor's big Smith and Wesson crept out its holster like a snake creeping from its lair. He held it at his side, listening while Sickert continued his harangue.

''You ain't never gonna get across the Borderlands to Chi before some Stormers or 'leps or Leather—''

BLAM! A big .44 slug cracked into Sickert's forehead. His voice stopped, his eyes bugged out, and he fell down, a nasty ooze of blood, brains, and bone chips staining the black asphalt where he lay sprawled.

''He was spreading low morale,'' said Vidor, slipping the still-smoking gun back into its leather resting place. ''Hey Dougal, you wanna be second on this patrol?''

Dougal really wanted to be first, but that would come. ''Sure,'' he said.

''Anyone else here think that taking all this for our own selves is a bad idea?''

The seventeen Stormers looked at Vidor, then over at Dougal, who fingered his Remington Autoloader, then down at Sickert's corpse. The back of his head was soaked in a pool of thick blood, the cold air making it heavy and oily, like lumpy gravy. His dirty hair swirled lazily in the red puddle.

''Well?'' demanded Vidor. ''What do you guys think?''

In the sullen silence that followed, the other Stormers looked at the ground or up at the tanks—they looked anywhere but at Vidor.

"Lennie!" yelled Vidor.

Lennie jumped.

"You think it's a good idea?"

Lennie pressed his thumb against his chest. "Me, boss?"

"How many Lennies we got?"

Lennie looked around as if hoping that another Stormer named Lennie might be handy. "One."

"So? Whaddya think?"

"Well, me, I . . . I think it's a fine idea," Lennie said with one eye on Sickert's stiffening corpse.

"Good," said Vidor, "then we all agree. I reckon all you guys agree with Lennie, right?"

"Okay," said Dougal, "this is what we're gonna do. Some of you head out and round up something we can put the gas in. Like barrels or something. The rest of us gotta figure out how to get the gas out of the tanks."

"Now hold on a piece," said Vidor. "I'm running this outfit."

"Just making a suggestion, boss," said Dougal.

"Oh, okay, that's different. Good idea. Barrels. I was just gonna mention that."

The group dispersed. A few men under Vidor's direction started ransacking the rusting sheds that stood in one corner of the tank site.

Dougal climbed up on one of the tanks and looked with confusion at the complicated system of valves that encircled the gas caps. All of the tanks were joined by a labyrinth of pipes, which led into one of the buildings that stood over near the old railway spur. Gas traveled through those pipes, but Dougal was damned if he knew how it all worked. He wasn't so much smart as he was cunning. Cunning was good, but smart was better. Smart men lived longer than cunning ones.

He hadn't figured he was going to have any trouble getting to the precious liquid inside all of those big old tanks. Somehow he thought that you just opened the top and scooped the stuff out, like a well. He was beginning to see that it wasn't that simple.

"Damn," he said, and kicked the metal under his feet. The tank boomed dully, as if mocking him. To make matters worse, just about then it started to rain; a cold, dirty rain. The icy drops were falling from the sky with startling speed, so he shot down the metal staircase, dashing for the cover of the old shacks. He kicked in the door and found Vidor and his men standing over an old gray metal desk closely examining something.

"Whassat?" demanded Dougal.

"Looky here," said Vidor with a leer. He held up an old calendar, yellowed around the edges. Each page was a different month and each month pictured a different woman. None of them wore clothes and they lazed about in languorous poses staring straight into the camera with a certain hot, smoky look in their eyes. Each page had, in addition, a rather stylized picture of a rabbit. "Ain't got nothing like this no more," breathed Vidor unhappily.

"You are crazy man," said Dougal, glancing coldly at the calendar. "We got work to do."

Vidor could feel his power slipping away from him. "We was just taking a break," he said meekly.

"Well, you gotta remember that we don't gotta a lotta time. Ole Leather could come down that road any minute."

"Jeez," said Vidor, paling slightly, "you think he could find us?"

"Maybe."

"So what you doing in here?" he said, suddenly trying to reassert his authority. "You're s'posed to be gettin' the gas."

"We gotta problem there," said Dougal evenly.

The Stormers spent the rest of the day, right up until nightfall robbed them of light, running up and down the tanks, pounding on the valves, trying to figure out how the whole system worked. They cussed and moaned and yelled in pain when they scraped pieces of their skin off on the rusty handles. By dark they were wet and unhappy and sure that they weren't going to see a drop of gas.

"We'll try tomorrow," said Dougal.

"Yeah," said Vidor, "great."

Long after dark, Lennie pushed off his dirty blanket and rolled out from under the rickety table that he had been sleeping beneath. Ranged around him in the room—it was the same one that had yielded up the calendar—were the muffled sleeping Stormers.

Lennie stretched, picked up his rusty Kassnar, and headed for the door.

Dougal sat upright in his tangle of bedding. "Where you going?" he hissed.

"Piss," said Lennie, yawning theatrically.

"With your rifle?"

"Who knows what's out there?"

"Leave it here."

"What? How come?"

"Cause I don't want anyone taking a hike."

"Where do you think I'm going? Listen to that shit." Rain was beating heavily on the tin roof of the shed.

"Leave the rifle."

Lennie shrugged and leaned the rifle against the wall. "Satisfied?"

"Don't take too long."

Outside, Lennie stood for a moment, cursing his luck. Dougal had guessed right. Lennie was getting out of there. He was heading straight back to Leather. But how far would he get without his gun? Well, one thing was for sure, he was leaving this bunch of fuck-ups behind. He walked away, the dark of the cold rainy night swallowing him in seconds.

Chapter Nineteen

In the cold, metallic light of morning Lennie saw very clearly that he had made a mistake. Sure, Vidor was dumb and Dougal was a murdering maniac but at least they possessed the means to survive—survive at least until they ran into Leather, that was. Once that happened he and his 'leps would slice up that sorry crew without even noticing almost. But right now they were in better shape than Lennie was. He was lost, cold, exhausted, hungry, and unarmed. The only thing he wasn't was thirsty—the rain had fallen all night and into the morning, soaking him to the bone.

He cursed himself for his hasty unplanned flight from Vidor. Wearily he sank down on the muddy ground and lowered his head into his hands. Tears welled up behind his eyes, mixing with the rainwater that already doused his face. He was going to die—he knew that, out here in the middle of nowhere, in the center of the black, inhospitable landscape that surrounded him. And it wouldn't be quick either. Slowly the cold and the hunger would gnaw at him but not before he became a walking skeleton, eaten away by exhaustion and hunger.

The wind whipped across his shoulders, as if by making him more uncomfortable it would hurt him more. A sudden cold flash of rainwater found its way down his collar and across his back, making him burn with a sudden anger.

"Goddammit!" he shouted, cursing the weather. He jerked his head back to scream some insults at the leaden sky. Instead, he screamed in fear. Standing above him were the Mean Brothers. They looked curiously at Lennie, as if they had discovered some strange new kind of life.

"Who the fuck are you?" said Lennie. He felt his stomach heave as if someone had suddenly cinched a belt tight around his middle. The agonizing death by cold and hunger suddenly looked pretty good. One of the Means took a step forward, wondering as he did so if he ought to kill this man.

"What," stammered Lennie, "what are you doing?"

The two Mean Brothers exchanged a look. The one closest to Lennie leaned down and grabbed the sorry Stormer by his sodden shirtfront. He heaved him up off the ground. He laid Lennie's scrawny body along his broad shoulders.

"Put me down!" screamed Lennie, kicking his feet and pounding his fists like a kid having a tantrum. He hit the Mean Brother as hard as he could but noticed that the blow had done about as much damage to the giant as it would have to a sheer rock face. The other Mean placed his finger against his lips as he tried to reason with Lennie to be quiet.

"Fuck you!" bawled Lennie, unable at that moment to think of anything more appropriate. At the back of his mind he believed that the Mean Brothers were not men at all but some kind of weird manlike animals that were going to take him back to their lair. To eat him, more than likely.

Almost apolegetically, the Mean Brothers smacked him in the side of the head, and blackness, like a hood, closed over him. . . .

As Lennie came to, he felt heat on his body and he thought: "I'm cooking." He was wrapped in a blanket as dirty as the one he had left behind in the shed on the tank site and was lying next to a fire.

Bonner, Starling, Beck, and J.B. stood over him. These guys were trouble, Lennie thought. He had never seen such a tough-looking foursome. No, tough wasn't the word: *dangerous*. That was it.

"So who are you, asshole?" asked Beck.

"Lennie," said Lennie meekly. "Are you guys Stormers?"

"You little prick," said Beck, reaching down to pull Lennie out of the sack and bat him around a little. Bonner stopped him.

"I guess that means no," said Lennie, smiling nervously.

"You a Stormer?" asked Bonner.

"Don't look like one," observed Starling.

"Sort of," said Lennie.

"Sort of," bellowed Beck. "Just what the hell does that mean?"

"I mean I used to be. I'm running now."

"If you were a Stormer, you too now a Stormer also, and I have only one thing for the Stormers and that is the fighting," said J.B. indignantly.

"Uh, what did he say?" asked Lennie.

"He doesn't like Stormers," said Bonner.

"But I told you," squealed Lennie, "I ain't no Stormer. I took off. Hell, even when I was with the Stormers I wasn't no Stormer, not really. Mister—" He turned to Bonner. He could sense that the Outrider had authority over the other men. "Mister, all I want to do is git off the road. I don't wanna fight nobody. I don't wanna kill nobody. . . ." Tears started into his eyes.

"So where were you headed?" Bonner asked.

"To the Cap," said Lennie, sniffing.

"You go to the Cap and Leather will cut your balls off for being a deserter," said Starling.

"No he won't," said Lennie quickly, "because—" He stopped suddenly.

"Why not?" asked Beck menacingly.

"Cause . . . cause . . ." Lennie stammered. He couldn't think of a good lie just then. Once upon a time Lennie considered himself a pretty fair liar.

''Time to kill the Stormer,'' said J.B. happily.

There was no doubt in Lennie's mind that J.B. meant what he said. The big northman took his heavy Browning pistol from his dirty fur coat and, cocking it, lowered the barrel until it was level with Lennie's eye.

''No! No! Wait!'' he screamed, trying to squirm away from the gun. He only had one card to play and he played it. ''Wait, I know about something you want. Gasoline, man, fucking more gasoline than you ever dreamed of.''

The four men exchanged glances. J.B. lowered his gun.

Lennie babbled on. ''Man, there must be twenty tanks. Full.''

''Where?'' said Bonner.

''Near here.''

''Where?''

''Man, it's straight back down the road. I walked away last night. It can't be far. . . .''

''Good. Now that we are knowing this thing he says, it is time now to shoot the Stormer dead in the head with my bullets.''

''C'mon man, that ain't fair,'' whined Lennie.

''Who found this place?'' asked Bonner, gently pushing aside the barrel of J.B.'s gun.

''My old Stormer troop.''

''Whose?'' asked Starling.

''Vidor's.''

''*Vidor* found the tank farm?'' asked Starling incredulously.

"He didn't believe it either," said Lennie. "It was sorta an accident."

"Where's he now?" asked Bonner.

"Still there. He 'n the others were going to load up and head out for Chi and keep the location secret. They wanted to double-cross Leather so I said hell, I'm getting out of here. Vidor can't take Leather. Vidor can't take down nobody."

"What you some kind of friend of Leather?" demanded Beck.

"Hell no. But like I said, Vidor's a fuck-up. Leather would slice him no problem. Probly wouldn't even notice. So I figured that I oughta get out and tell Leather and Leather would be grateful."

"I think you're telling the truth, sonny," said Starling.

"I *know* I am."

"Time to move, Bonner," said Beck.

"I think you're right."

"What about him?" asked Starling.

"*Now* is the time to shoot, yes?"

"Hell," said Bonner, "why not just leave him."

"He's helped us a lot," put in Starling.

"Awww Bonner," said J.B. "You have the heart of a baby."

Lennie watched Bonner's little convoy move out onto the road. There was Bonner in the lead in his heavy machine, Beck and Starling on their bikes, and the Habitants' big truck bringing up the rear. Lennie was extremely glad that he wasn't going to be at the tank farm when that crowd showed up. Vidor and

Dougal and the rest would never know what hit
them. Bonner disappeared over the rise in the road
and Lennie picked up the food that he had been given
and started walking quickly in the opposite direction.
Around about midday he was captured by Radleps.
After a hour or so of pleading for his life, he was
taken to see Leatherman.

Bonner and company looked down on the tank
farm from the high vantage point of one of the steep
valley sides. Bonner, Beck, Starling, and the Habitants stared down as though they were parched desert
travelers who had finally found an oasis. Bonner
recalled the words that had been spoken to him so
many months ago by Cooker, the gas hound who had
originally discovered the tank farm: "I found the
promised land," He cackled. He was right.

Bonner ran his eye over the tank farm spread out
beneath him. All of the tanks were joined by pipes
leading into a central pump house. Cooker had known
how to operate the whole setup—and he had dropped
big hints about its workings to Bonner.

"Plenty there for everybody," said Starling.

"All you have to do is get rid of them," said
Bonner, pointing to the center of the site. Standing
there were the Stormers of Vidor's patrol. They were
watching as Vidor and Dougal had an argument.
Bonner was too far off to hear their angry words, but
the argument was a fierce one: the two men stamped
and waved their arms and shook their fists at one
another. Suddenly, Dougal whipped out a pistol and
shot Vidor, much as Vidor had shot Sickert the day

before. The single shot echoed in the cold air and a faint pall of blue smoke drifted skyward. The Stormers winced at the sound of the blast.

Vidor hit the ground, apparently dead. Dougal turned his attention to the rest of the Stormers and started yelling at them. Just then, Vidor appeared to revive a little. He lifted his right arm off the ground and fired two shots into the back of Dougal's head. That done, he died. A second or two later, Dougal followed him.

The remaining Stormers looked at each other for a second or two, then began jabbering away at one another, presumably about what to do. After a few minutes they ran to their beat-up old bikes and took off, roaring up the far side of the valley as fast as they could.

"Again there are no Stormers for the killing," said J.B. disgustedly.

"Let's go get that shit," said Beck, angling his heavy cycle down the steep road.

Bonner followed. He wondered where Leather was.

Chapter Twenty

Seth had agreed to follow them up the valley at his own pace. It wasn't much after midday when his big locomotive steamed onto the railway spur that once served the tank farm.

Bonner was standing next to the track as Seth switchbacked his engine around. The blunt nose of the engine was facing down the valley the way he had come. The three tanker cars were drawn up next to the filling nozzles that arched next to the track. There were large conduit pipes that fit neatly into the filler caps in the tank cars.

"Wish I had two more cars," said Seth, gesturing toward the pipes. "Five pipes we got. Coulda filled five cars."

"No sense in getting greedy," said Bonner.

"You having trouble getting the stuff out?"

"A little. The pump station doesn't work. Starling and J.B. took the thing apart. The motor is fine, just needs cleaning."

Seth looked around him and whistled softly. "Sure is a hell of a lot of it. Looks like we'll be coming back here for quite a piece of time."

"I doubt it," said Bonner. He explained briefly about the fleeing remnants of Vidor's column.

"So it's not a secret no more," said Seth. "Too bad."

A snort of smoke belched from a stack over the pumping station, followed by the coughing of rusty old machinery. It clattered for a moment, then died. Bonner and Seth could hear J.B. bellowing curses in his native tongue. A few moments of silence followed, then the engine burst into prolonged, high-revving life. Starling emerged from the pit, wiping dirty grease from his hands.

"Well, it's going. I don't know how long it will last though."

"Okay," said Bonner. "We're gonna drain number-one tank. That's that one. I don't think Seth can take much more than half of that."

"So how does it work?"

"Close all the valves on the other tanks. Open number one and start the pumps. At least, that's how I think it works. . . ."

"We'll have to work the valves by hand," said Starling.

"No problem," said Bonner.

Men fanned out across the tank farm. There were a lot of valves but there were more men. Men took their stations next to a valve wheel at some point along the rusty pipes that connected all of the tanks with each other and the release pipes on the railway siding.

Seth stood guard over the train ready to signal when the tank cars were filled with the precious golden fluid. There was probably a gauge someplace that would do just that for him but he didn't know where it was. Bonner was in the pump house ready to engage the pump mechanism once the appropriate valves had been opened.

Starling stood at the base of the number-one tank and grasped the main petcock.

"Starling!" shouted Bonner.

"Yo?"

"Ready?"

"Any time."

"Then open it."

"Right." Starling leaned into the wheel and grunted with the force of his effort. But it wouldn't budge. "Bonner! Hold it. I need some help getting this thing going."

Louis, the little Hab, understood the meaning of Starling words. He trotted out from the cab of the Habs' truck to lend a hand, his scarred and nasty-looking rifle in his hands. He made a short speech in his crazy language to Starling, testifying to his great strength.

"Okay, Frenchie," said Starling with an amused

grin. "Let's do it." Louis spat on his red, gnarled hands and laid hold of the valve wheel. Both men dug their heels into the ground and twisted. For a second nothing happened, then slowly, with a sound like the grinding of gears, the rusty wheel turned.

"Go," shouted Starling.

Bonner threw the pump into gear, the other valves opened, and within a minute or two the site was suffused with the sweet smell of gasoline. Some of the old pipes were split and corroded, and sprang leaks. Little rivers of gasoline raced around the cracked asphalt, but they didn't lower the pressure enough to keep the gas from dribbling into Seth's tanks. He heard the gasoline hitting the steel bottom of the tank cars and he smiled to himself.

Bonner stood in the pump room with Beck.

"Well, we got this shit for good," observed Beck happily.

"Yeah," said Bonner. The old world was staring him in the face. He was busy examining the array of dials and gauges that had once indicated something to somebody. Bonner couldn't be sure but it looked as if once all of the valves could have been opened automatically and the gas moved around the site by a single man sitting behind the controls. None of the needles danced and the gauges represented nothing now as the gas slowly drained out of number-one tank. They had been broken years before, probably bombed out of whack by the jolting earthquakes when the bombs crashed down to earth.

Seth could only tell how full the tanks were by the

sound of the gas pouring in. As the thundering note within the steel confines changed from low to middle to high he could tell he was getting close to full. He waited a minute or two then called out.

"Hold it!"

Bonner shut down the pump and the valley was silent. Or almost silent. Grinding up the road that ran next to the murky stream that split the valley was Leatherman and his 'lep battalion.

The force of inertia in the pipes kept the gas coming for a second or two and a fine fountain of the stuff splashed over the tops of the tanks and soaked the ground around them. But no one noticed. The men on the site had paused, standing still, listening to the inexorable roar of the engines of their enemies.

"A fighting now," said J.B. happily.

"Bonner!" shouted Starling. Number-one tank was on the far side of the site, closest to the onrushing Radleps.

"I see 'em. Seth!"

"Yeah?"

"Your loco fired and ready to go?"

"Yep."

"Then take off."

"Where we going to meet?"

"Chi. Move it." Bonner was darting from the pump house, looking for the right defensive position. They were going to have to slow down the 'leps if they could.

Seth climbed up to the cab of his train. He tugged on the throttle and looked out over the site. Leatherman had brought a lot of friends. All Bonner could do was fire enough shots to make them keep their heads down for a few minutes, then beat it the hell out of there. The train began easing itself down the railroad as if it was an old lady with all the time in the world. Then the heavy tanks behind him grabbed the down-grade of the track and began pushing the locomotive along the rails.

Leatherman had Chilly pull the jeep up on the side of the road. That was as far as he was going. He wasn't a coward but he knew his fighting days were over. He consoled himself by reminding himself that he would never fire another shot in anger—but his killing days were far from done. Lennie sat in the backseat, incredibly proud that he was going to watch the battle from Leatherman's jeep.

Leather pulled himself from his seat and leaned on the windshield. The Radleps screamed past like a long trail of angry hornets. They were headed di-rectly for the old Cyclone-fence gates of the tank park. Leather watched them pass like a general re-viewing his troops.

He saw Seth's train move slowly off the site. Leather wanted it all. He wanted the gas, he wanted Bonner, he might as well take Seth too. He flagged down some of the passing Radleps.

"Get me that train," he ordered.

The 'lep nodded and obediently a piece of the force sliced off the main body and took off after Seth.

Bonner knew it was a battle he couldn't win. The

'leps were roaring onto the site seventy, maybe a hundred strong. His own force was twenty or so men and they were scattered throughout the acreage of the tank farm. A couple were up on the tanks; the rest were down on the ground, digging in for the fierce confrontation that was about to erupt.

Bonner sprinted to his car and picked up the AUG, noticing as he did so that the blunt-ass end of Seth's train was disappearing around the bend in the track with a squad of Radleps in hot pursuit. From the far side of the tank farm came the sound of shots being fired. The struggle had begun.

The 'leps had flooded onto the tank site, filling the narrow valley with engine noise. Bonner dashed up the metal stairs of one of the tanks and braced himself against the railing. The sharp snout of the AUG waved over the ground below and began to chatter, cutting down 'leps with surgical precision. The barrel coughed and spat flame and hot lead into the bodies of the brave but foolish half men who rushed by below him. A passing 'lep took a brace of bullets in the head, blasting a furious fountain of gore into the air. His bike cracked up at the base of a tank.

The Mean Brothers perched on a tank stairway, tensed and ready to jump the thirty feet to the ground. A 'lep pulled by them, stopped, and pushed back the goggles that protected his eyes. A Mean silently launched himself into the air, his ax held firmly in one hand. He dropped from the sky, his huge feet thumping directly onto the 'lep's shoulders. The weight of the Mean Brother, coupled with the distance he had dropped, was too much for the delicate bones of the Radlep's shoulders. There was a sound of the tearing of bone and gristle, mixed with the passionate scream of pain of the unfortunate man, and he seemed to split apart. He fell off his Honda, his voice raised high and hot with a wail of pain. He couldn't move his arms to grab for the gun in his belt: the force of the Mean Brother's blow had forever severed the bones and muscles of his upper back.

The Mean was disappointed. He had hoped the Radlep would put up more of a fight. Perfunctorily he swung his ax and felt no satisfaction when the blade chopped into the 'lep's broken body. There was no sport in carving up a paralyzed man. But a job was a job. . . .

Beck idly wondered what to do. He had unslung his little machine pistol; the tiny gun looked microscopic in his huge hands. Plainly there were too many 'leps for them to take down. Besides, Seth had already steamed out of the gas yard, so there was no need to stay. The prudent Beck told him that it was time to go. The wild-man Beck hated to leave a fight.

"What the hell," he said, "I'll stay for a minute or two." He squeezed the trigger of his gun, blistering the foul skin off the chest of a passing 'lep. The 'lep flew off his bike, and as he hit the cold ground he smashed a number of bones in his abdomen and thighs, but he squirmed a yard or two to the cover of a tank, almost swimming there in his blood. He unslung his M16 as he went. The pain pulsed through his tortured body but it was nothing compared to his driving desire to kill the big man that had brought him down. He clenched his broken teeth, trying to fight off the agony long enough to get a clear, steady shot at Beck. But his whole body was screaming out for help—tortured nerves were sending urgent messages all along his shattered nervous system, demanding that his brain attend to their wants immediately. The first shots at Beck went way wide.

"You fucks don't know when to lie down, do you?" yelled Beck, directing a stream of yellow fire at the 'lep. The man jumped a little as the sharp bullets sliced into him. Blood spurted from him like a fountain and he died, crazy mad that he had not killed the man who had brought him down.

Leather watched the battle dispassionately. By his reckoning he had already lost ten men. Only one force fought that hard against Radleps. Bonner was down there, cutting down Leather's men. Bonner was unafraid of their fierce reputation. A 'lep was just another enemy. Bonner killed his enemies.

A heavy .44 slug slapped against the railing that Bonner leaned against. He was drawing fire from somewhere. Another bullet danced at his feet. The next one wouldn't miss. He darted up the stairs a few feet, sweeping the ground below him with the hot muzzle of the Steyr AUG. Then he saw a lone 'lep crouching behind a pile of rusty pipes, taking careful aim with a long bore rifle. The AUG spat, tearing the Radlep's face into a messy slimy stew. Pieces of nose and cheekbone flew around his head as if suddenly stirred up by a hot murderous wind.

Bullets were flattening themselves against rusty tanks and Bonner knew it was only a matter of time before a powerful high-caliber shell found a weak spot in the thin metal hide and blew. Time to get out. The man nearest him was J.B. happily murdering Radleps.

"J.B.," yelled Bonner.

J.B. looked down the barrel of his gun and blasted a 'lep out of the saddle of his Harley. *"Oui?"*

"I think"—Bonner whipped his cutdown blaster from its holster and tore a Radlep to shreds—"it's time to go."

"I am also thinking this," screamed J.B.

"Beck!"

"I heard you, man."

"Starling!"

Starling and Louis were on the far side of the tank ground, near the gate. The little Hab's heavy hammer had smacked the barrel of his gun again and again, cutting down anything in the path of the wide mouth that vomited steel and fire. Starling hadn't been using his arrows. He knew that his steel shafts would easily penetrate one of the tanks and send the whole place up. His own Steyr was performing the same task as Bonner's. Together, Starling and Louis had piled up quite a large heap of broken bikes and Radleps. But enough had gotten by him. They had established themselves more or less in the middle of the camp, cutting Starling and Louis off from the far side of the valley, from Bonner and safety. Starling suddenly realized that this was going to be one firefight it was going to be tough to get out of.

All at once, the shooting stopped. The 'leps had dismounted now and were crawling around looking for riders. The rest of the battle would be fought hand to hand.

"Starling!" shouted Bonner.

"What?"

"Where are you?"

"Next to the gate."

Bonner swore silently. Starling couldn't be in a worse place. He was far away and the bulk of the 'lep force sat between him and Bonner.

"We'll come and get you," yelled Bonner.

Starling waited a moment before replying.

"Don't be an asshole, Bonner. Me 'n Frenchy got plans of our own. You head up the valley and we'll meet you in Chi."

Bonner knew that Starling knew that he was a dead man.

"Starling," yelled Bonner.

"Beat it, Bonner. I'll see you at Dorca's."

"Starling!" yelled Bonner again.

"Goddammit!" Starling's angry voice echoed across the smoky gas yard. "I always did what you told me to. You were always the boss. I followed the orders, on account of you being smarter than me, okay? But this time, man, do what I say. Move it. Got it?"

J.B. grabbed Bonner by the shoulder. "He will be fine, okay? He has Louis with him. Now we go, yes?"

Bonner slid behind the wheel, and just before he fired up he heard Starling's voice.

"Bonner? Get Leather for me. One day, okay? You get him."

Leather heard the threat and smiled at Chilly. "No fuckin' way," said Leather.

That's a promise, thought Bonner.

"Let's go," bellowed Beck.

As Bonner and company moved off, racing up the far side of the valley, the 'lep force split in two. One half jumped for their bikes and began following the riders up the steep valley sides. A Hab had jumped into the back of Bonner's car and cocked the big machine gun; he stared down the barrel for a second and with a Mean Brother feeding ammo began peppering their pursuers with big, tearing bullets. The Habs in the back of their truck took up the fire and cut into the 'leps who struggled to ride their bikes up the hill and fire at the same time. They were good, but they weren't that good. In the closing minutes of the battle the riders took down another eleven 'leps. A good day's work.

Starling watched his friends battle their way up the side of the valley. They were going to make it. He knew he wasn't. So what, he said to himself. He had nothing else to do really. A few more drinks at Dorca's, a few more rides . . . That's all. He'd miss Bonner and Beck too, the big fuck. . . . But it was better this way. Let Bonner get away. Bonner had work to do. He had to kill Leather. If anyone was going to do it, it was Bonner. . . .

"Okay, Frenchy, it's just you and me."

"Yez," said Louis.

A 'lep peeped around a corner and Louis smacked his gun with a hammer and the 'lep turned instantly into a hanging curtain of blood, bone, and juice.

"If they come at us one at a time, we might have a chance," said Starling optimistically.

But they didn't come one at a time. Starling and Louis were flat-backed against one of the tanks when twenty 'leps rushed them. Louis's terrible gun cut down a few, but Starling didn't bother. He unslung his bow, turned his back on the charging 'leps, and pulled back the bowstring. The sharp point of the deadly arrow was aimed point-blank at the skin of the tank.

"Bye, Frenchy. Sorry I said anything about your gun there. She's a beaut."

"*Au revoir*, Starling," said Louis.

The steel point cut through the rusty side of the fuel tank and detonated inside. An enormous ball of flame exploded into the gray day like a second sun. The fire enveloped Starling and Louis, killing them instantly. The wave of flame washed across the park, frying the 'leps in their own fat, and then swept on, reaching another tank. That one blew, setting off another, fire spiraling up into the dirty sky, bright like the Bomb itself. . . .

Bonner had reached the top of the valley and looked back. The tank site was a swirling sea of flame, a raging vortex of fire so strong he could feel the heat hot and tight on his face. One mile away, on

the far side of the valley, Leather watched his gasoline and his 'leps burn. Bonner was too far off to
make out the expression on the Leatherman's face,
but he could see the fire glinting bright on Leather's
metal hands.

Chapter Twenty-one

Seth beat it down the valley as fast as he could, knowing that he was going to have to squeeze every ounce of power he could out of his old black steam giant if he was going to stand a chance of outrunning the Radleps on his tail. He had a fair head start but he knew that the bikes the 'leps rode were perfectly capable of eating away the distance between him and them in no time flat. He was in bullet range now, and he half expected to hear shots. A single clean M16 round into his cargo tanks and he would be dead before the flames burned his hair down to his scalp.

Power. He needed more power. He kicked open the heavy iron door of the boiler furnace and turned with his usual strength and economy of movement to the filling of the inferno with coal. A dozen strokes with the shovel pumped a half ton of the black rocks onto the fire, and he felt his locomotive seize the added fuel and strain to race a little bit faster. The stack belched black smoke and the great iron pistons pounded with the effort to reach the power that Seth demanded.

His machine pistol was slung over the brake handle and he grabbed it, cradling it against his stomach. He chanced a quick look off to the side of the foot plate and saw Radleps—a lot, thirty or so—crouched low over their handlebars, sweeping up along side. These men weren't dumb like the Stormers he had encountered earlier in his trip; they didn't back up behind the roaring tonnage of the rail-borne behemoth; instead they rode close to the tank cars, guessing that Seth wouldn't risk trying to cut them down with a spray of automatic fire for fear that just one of his bullets would go wide and slam into the brimming fuel tanks.

As he leaned out to take a look, a single shot from a handgun whistled past his ear. The 'leps figured that as long as they were shooting forward of the tanks, they didn't have to worry too much about stray bullets. In other words, Seth was a target, but they weren't.

By now it had become plain to him that they wanted the train whole and intact. If they only wanted him dead, they would have fallen back to a safe distance and sent their big shells racing forward to blow him out of the cold morning. They wanted the gas. When they had it, they would kill him.

Seth hunched on the foot plate, wondering what he could do to save himself, when up behind his shoulder he saw a single Radlep standing on the coal heaped just behind the engine in the tender. Obviously, he had abandoned his bike somewhere behind and had climbed over the gas tanks, his M16 held ready to bring Seth down. Brave man, thought Seth as his quick M3A sent a stern message of death to the 'lep's tall thin body. His leather jacket shredded under the hot hailstorm of bullets. He fell onto the coal pile, red blood pulsing out onto the black shiny rocks.

Seth ignored him as he bent to throw some more coal on his engine fire.

Under cover of the noise of the shovel and the thunderous pumping of the pistons, a 'lep pulled himself up next to the foot plate. He held his bike steady for a moment then swung himself off the screaming machine, jumping for the grab bar running next to the steep steel steps that ran up the side of the locomotive. The riderless bike stood erect for a moment then fell over, its engine racing.

The Radlep scrambled onto the train and lunged at Seth, grabbing him around the waist. Seth's nostrils filled with the dirty rotting stench that some of the 'leps gave off as their bodies slowly turned to a mass of putrefaction. Seth grappled with the man, feeling the curious slide and shift of the man's body under his clothes as great plates of skin tore and sliced. It was as if the man was coming apart at the seams and made him feel like he was bathed in oil.

But the 'lep fought like a man in the peak of

health. His strong fingers closed around Seth's throat, and they flexed, the force of his squeeze causing a dozen scabs on his joints to break. Clear liquid mixed with an oily pus flowed out of the newly opened wounds, and Seth felt the viscous fluid drain onto his face and neck, trickling down underneath his shirt. He shivered in revulsion. The horror of the Radlep and his hideous wounds brought forth a surge of strength in Seth. He shot a knee up quickly into the 'lep's groin, doubling him over in pain.

Seth picked up his shovel and swung, catching the Radlep on the side of the head. Instantly the oily flesh swelled and closed an eye. The scarred warrior immediately grabbed for the big Llama Automatic that he wore at his side. But before he could pull it from his belt Seth swung again, and the 'lep felt the sharp reverberation of the steel shovel as it met the hard bones on his face. His head was a mass of blood. He fell.

Another Radlep was knocking on the door. He was climbing up the iron steps, pulling himself aboard with one hand and wielding a long deadly-looking machete in the other.

Seth lunged with the shovel, rapping the man on the knuckles, then aiming a kick straight into the center of the 'lep's chest. The force of the blow stunned him and he toppled back toward the open side of the train and the rushing landscape beyond. Just in time, before falling, he grabbed for the metal rail, dropping the knife as he did so. Seth reared back and beat the 'lep's hands with the shovel, swinging again and again like a lumberjack at the base of a tall tree.

The 'lep's cracked lips opened wide and he screamed in agony. Again the shovel landed on his tortured hands, and Seth could imagine the the man's hands turning into bloody stumps of bone and skin inside the stout leather gloves that he wore. Seth grabbed all the strength he could find in his body and slammed a final blow against the man's meaty hand: it seemed to squash the flesh flat against the iron of the locomotive's side. With a pain-wracked wail the Radlep, unable to stand the fierce torment, unable to absorb one more blow, let go. Seth didn't watch him fall. He turned and scooped up the body of the bloody Radlep who still cluttered the foot plate, and tossed him off the rushing train to join his brother warrior. The body of the 'lep bounced on the rocky ground when he hit.

The remaining 'leps had fallen behind a bit, as if they wanted time to contemplate their next move. Seth slammed the throttle full open and immediately managed to add to the little bit of daylight between him and his pursuers. He had to act soon. Not too far ahead the track left the gentle grade of the valley floor and began its long slow ascent up the steep side of the valley. The iron horse would have to slow down to almost a walking pace if it was going to haul its heavy load up that incline—if he cut speed that much, the 'leps would be all over him.

He had about three miles in which to make his move. A tunnel was looming up ahead, its great black mouth yawning wide to swallow him and his short train up. A plan formed like a pearl within his mind. He climbed out onto the side of the fuel tank that rode just behind the engine. As he went he prayed that the 'leps hadn't taken up positions on both sides of the train. He was so exposed that he knew that if a 'lep marksman saw him, he would take a chance on a single shot to whip Seth off his precarious foothold on the side of the tank car. But he was safe. The 'leps were bunched together on the far side of the train.

Seth crawled to the joint between the first and the second tank cars. He paused for a moment, trying not to look at the ground that blurred by him. He gathered his strength and then hurled himself across the wide opening between the two cars, landing neatly on the opposite narrow deck of the second car. From there he inched his way down the length of the tank and finally reached his objective.

He swung himself in between the two cars and turned the brake wheel that would slow down the third car. Then he pulled the lynching pin from its place on the side of the tank car. With this long piece of metal hooked at one end he reached down, as if fishing, and unhooked the heavy metal coupling that bound the second car to the third. He swatted at the rubber hose of the brake coupling and severed the old rubber with a single blow. The last car had been cut free now and was still moving rapidly, carried along by the stored speed of the whole train and the weight of the fuel in the tank.

Seth was running out of time now. He couldn't afford the time to take the safe way back, inching along the far side of the cars to the relative safety of the control center of the locomotive. He had to run for it, taking the quickest route: back across the top of the tanks. He took a deep breath, like a swimmer before a dive into icy-cold water, then he hauled himself up to the top of the car. He ran across the slippery tanks as fast as he could. His heavy boots rang on the metal. The 'leps saw him but no one chanced a shot.

Seth dived off the top and fell into the coal pile just behind the foot plate. He lay there a second, his chest heaving, gulping in air. The tunnel was up ahead. Behind him the 'leps were looking curiously at the lone tank car that was rolling along, now quite far behind the train, looking like an ungainly calf chasing after its mother.

Black enveloped him as the train swept into the tunnel. The pulsing noise of the engine was doubled in intensity as it bounced and ricocheted off the walls. Seth stared behind him as the drifting tank car entered the tunnel with the Radleps just behind it. They slowed down to squeeze by the car as it took up most of the width of the tunnel. When Seth judged that most of the 'leps were caught in the narrow alley between the tank's steel sides and the unforgiving brick of the tunnel, he let rip with a half-dozen slugs, each one slicing into the lake of gasoline.

The noise of the explosion was deafening, and flames raced out in all directions. The air was thick with fire, smoke, and pieces of tank and Radleps. Seth had thrown himself flat on the foot plate, half expecting some fiery piece of shrapnel to tear through the air and pierce the delicate skin of the remaining tanks.

The train rushed out into the light. Behind Seth the mouth of the tunnel swirled with smoke, and it looked like the barrel of a giant shotgun that had just fired a mammoth charge. Of the Radleps there was no sign. Their torn bodies were strewn around the track at the entrance to the tunnel, now just sticky piles of flesh all burning brightly.

Seth lit a cigar and tugged the throttle down for the long hard slow climb out of the valley.

Seth exhaled and smiled to himself, thinking of what Beck would say when he showed up in Chicago with two tanks instead of three. No, Beck was not going to be pleased at all.

Epilogue

Bonner battled a snowstorm most of the way back to Chicago. The Mean Brothers crouched in the back of the car, dozing most of the way, getting out only when Bonner needed their vast strength to pull his tortured vehicle clear of a heavy snowdrift.

J.B. and the Habs were somewhere behind him. They all planned to meet in the city and divide up the spoils when Seth arrived.

Chi was cold and quiet when Bonner arrived deep in the night. He woke up Lucky, who grumbled about being disturbed and the cold and a lot of other things.

"I'll bet you fucked up your automobile too," he said acidly.

"Yeah," said Bonner, "probably."

"As fucking usual. Did you get the gas?"

"Yeah. We got it."

"Well at least you did something right. Not much gas around these days. You'll be earning yourself quite a heap of slates."

Bonner walked through the snow-blown streets. It was too cold for even the lowliest street worker to be out looking for an easy bringdown like a vulture. The lights were on at Dorca's, but the usual ruckus didn't spill out into that unfriendly night. The world was asleep, thought Bonner, or dead.

He walked wearily up the four flights of stairs that led to his book-lined lair. He swung open the door and called into the darkness.

"It's me."

He heard the girl put down the shotgun that he knew she had leveled at him. A second later she raced out of the darkness and enfolded him in her arms. She smelled warm and clean, and suddenly he caught the acid smell of his own unwashed and exhausted body.

"Are you hurt?" she asked.

"No."

"Tired?"

"They got Starling."

Good, she thought. Kill them all. Kill all these damn adventurers who lured Bonner out onto the road with vows of friendship and tales of riches.

Bonner lowered himself onto the bed. He could feel the warmth where her body had lain waiting for him. In his mind he took down the ledger in which he kept the list of scores to be settled. To the cruel death of Dara and the fiery demise of Cooker and Harvey, Bonner now added a new name: Starling. An Outrider. Dead for a few gallons of gas.

The tiny flames of mercy and forgiveness that burned within the Outrider guttered and died. As they were snuffed out, the furnace of hate and revenge in his heart grew hotter—as hot as the flames of hell that Leather would one day suffer. Bonner would be the one that sent him there. That he swore silently on the names and memories of his dead friends.

The girl snuggled down at his side. Safe.

Watch for

BLOOD HIGHWAY

third novel in the new
OUTRIDER series

coming in November!